THE EAGLE AND THE WREN

THE EAGLE AND THE WREN

Jeanne Whitmee

Chivers Press • Thorndike Press
Bath, England   Thorndike, Maine USA

This Large Print edition is published by Chivers Press, England, and by Thorndike Press, USA.

Published in 2000 in the U.K. by arrangement with the author.

Published in 2000 in the U.S. by arrangement with Dorian Literary Agency.

U.K. Hardcover   ISBN 0–7540–4078–X (Chivers Large Print)
U.K. Softcover   ISBN 0–7540–4079–8 (Camden Large Print)
U.S. Softcover   ISBN 0–7862–2470–3 (General Series Edition)

The text of this Large Print edition is unabridged.
Other aspects of the book may vary from the original edition.

Set in 16 pt. New Times Roman.

Printed in Great Britain on acid-free paper.

British Library Cataloguing in Publication Data available

Library of Congress Cataloging-in-Publication Data

Whitmee, Jeanne.
    The eagle and the wren / by Jeanne Whitmee.
       p. cm.
    ISBN 0–7862–2470–3 (lg. print : sc : alk. paper)
    1. France—History—Revolution, 1789–1799—Refugees—Fiction.
    2. Refugees—England—Dorset—Fiction. 3. Dorset (England)
    —Fiction. 4. Large type books.   I. Title.
PR6073.H65 E25   2000
823'.914—dc21   99–087730

CHAPTER ONE

Daylight was beginning to fade as the London coach rattled into Dorchester. All was bustle in the yard of the King's Head but at first Abigail Labeque and her two travelling companions were too stiff and tired to take any interest. Abigail alighted while Sister Ursula did her best to rouse the elderly Sister Joseph who had been snoring loudly these past two hours.

The evening air was warm and mellow and Abigail breathed deeply and gratefully, stretching her cramped limbs. It was 10 a.m. when they left Salisbury and the convent. Nine long hours they had rattled together in the coach with Sister Joseph complaining and sleeping by turns—both equally noisily. Sister Ursula had remained quiet, glancing wistfully at Abigail from time to time. She was the nearest to a child of her own that she had ever had and this parting would be a wrench for both of them.

But as she stood on the cobbles of the inn yard, Abigail's thoughts were not of sadness or of parting. Through the open gates she could glimpse the little stone houses, so different from the older timbered buildings of Salisbury, and her heart gave a little skip of excitement as she realized that very soon now she would enter into her new life at Broomcott Manor.

It would be a very different life from that which she left behind her at the convent, that much was certain—but what *would* it be like? Her great uncle, Thomas Hargreaves—would he be as she had pictured him: a rosy-faced country gentleman, good-humoured and always ready with a kind word—something like Father Jeremy, the priest at St. Dominic's?

Abigail had been at St. Dominic's Convent ever since her mother died when she was seven years old. Her French father, Pierre Labeque, had decided that it would be best for her. A Paris wine merchant's house was no place for a motherless child and besides, there was growing unrest in the city. Sometime soon he foresaw that there would be trouble, and he was right. The revolution had raged for three long years now. All France seemed to have gone mad. Abigail had not seen her father since the summer of 1788 when she had been fourteen. Together they had spent a holiday with friends in the beautiful wine country of Provence. After her return to the convent his letters had grown shorter and more infrequent, till finally, they had stopped altogether. Then had come that terrible day a month ago when she had been called to Mother Angela's room and told gently that her Papa was dead. It seemed he had been arrested, accused, like so many other innocent people, of being an 'enemy of the revolution' and condemned to death at the hands of the dreaded Judge Fouquier Tinville.

Although she had seen little of her Papa over the past few years, Abigail wept bitterly for him. How could a man as good and kind as he be an enemy of any kind? Now she had no one in the world. What was to become of her? But a letter deposited fortuitously by Pierre Labeque at an English bank showed otherwise. He had left instructions that it should be sent to Abigail in the event of his demise. Abigail's mother, it seemed, had one living relative residing in England. An uncle, Thomas Hargreaves, who was Squire of the village of Broomcott in the county of Dorset. He had undertaken to care for and provide for Abigail in the event of her father's death, until such time as she married or came of age when she would inherit money left in trust for her. So it was that she stood here in the yard of the King's Head now, waiting for the servant her uncle was sending to accompany her to Broomcott Manor.

A boy loaded down with boxes brushed against Abigail, causing her to stumble and Sister Ursula caught her arm.

'Do you swoon, child?'

Abigail smiled up into the gentle face of the tall nun. 'No, I feel better now that I have breathed fresh air and stretched myself.' She looked round anxiously. 'I wonder where the man is who is to take me to my uncle?' They

3

scanned the faces of the bustling throng in the yard, but no one seemed to be looking for them.

'Mother of God! I swear that every bone in my body is broken!' Sister Joseph climbed down from the coach with surprising agility and frowned at them crossly, but Sister Ursula shook her head.

'It does not seem right that we should hand the child over in this arbitrary way. I think we should accompany her the rest of the way to Broomcott and satisfy ourselves that she is safe.'

Sister Joseph's face fell, but at that moment a man in a plain brown cloth coat and leather breeches stepped up to them, doffing his wide-brimmed hat respectfully.

'Pardon me, ladies, but would this be Miss Abigail Labeque?'

Abigail turned to the man excitedly. 'Yes—I am Abigail Labeque. Have you come from my Uncle Thomas Hargreaves?'

The man nodded. 'I have that, Miss. If you'll show me which are your boxes we'll make a start. I've got the wagon waiting.'

When the Sisters saw the farm wagon the man pointed out they were dismayed.

'What does the man think she is—a peasant?' Sister Joseph said indignantly. 'It looks to me as though it had recently transported pigs!' She wrinkled her nose. 'Huh! It smells as though it had too!'

4

But Sister Ursula's worries were of a more serious nature. 'Have you not brought a female chaperon for our charge,' she asked the man, 'and what if you should meet with cut-purses on the way? I really think that we should accompany you to Broomcott.'

The man, Jed Harker, was perplexed. He'd been told to bring the young lady only—and the Lord knew there'd been enough chuntering over that! It was clear that the poor young miss wasn't what you'd call welcome at Broomcott if he was to turn up with two ladies of the veil too, he hardly dared think what his master would say. He didn't hold much with the church let alone popery! Jed scratched his head.

'If you'll pardon me, Miss—er—Ma'am,' he said hesitantly. 'One lady will be enough for me to protect. Three, I'd be afeared to manage.'

'Of course, the man's perfectly right!' Sister Joseph interjected. 'What good d'you think *we'd* be against cut-purses? We'd only encourage them to attack us all the harder!'

Sister Ursula looked at the elderly nun doubtfully. She knew Sister Joseph was tired, needing a bed and hot food and it was part of her duty to see that she got both. She glanced at Abigail's face. The girl's brown eyes were bright and her cheeks rosy with excitement. From under her travelling hood tendrils of curling dark hair were escaping endearingly.

Sister Ursula sighed. Once she had hoped that the child might take vows, but as she had grown to womanhood it became clear that a life of seclusion was not for her. She belonged to the world and needed the company of others of her own age and disposition. She took so poignantly after her mother, Anne Hargreaves, who had also been educated at St. Dominic's and had been Ursula's closest girlhood friend. She smiled gently, stepping up to Abigail and taking the small pointed face between her long hands.

'You will be all right, child? If you are afraid we will accompany you. You have only to ask.'

But Abigail shook her head, her eyes enormous with excitement, yet a shiver of delicious apprehension making her tremble. 'I'll be quite all right,' she assured the Sister. 'The man looks trustworthy enough. Please don't worry about me. Take care of poor Sister Joseph. She looks so tired.'

The tall nun bent and kissed her on both cheeks. 'Be good and obedient to your uncle, child. And remember your prayers.'

'I will, I will,' Abigail told her, 'and I'll write to Mother Angela the moment I get to Broomcott. Oh, Sister Ursula!' Her voice broke as a sudden sob rose in her throat and she threw her arms round the nun. 'I'll miss you *so* much. You won't forget me, will you?'

'I will always be with you in spirit, child, never fear. You will be in my thoughts and prayers always.'

Jed Harker cleared his throat. 'If you're ready, Miss, I think we should be making a start—if you please.' He doffed his hat again. 'Your boxes be all loaded.'

Hurriedly Abigail kissed Sister Ursula again and briefly embraced Sister Joseph who wished her good fortune gruffly. Then with Jed's help she mounted the wagon and drew her cloak closely round her. What fun to be travelling like this! It never occurred to her to wonder why her uncle had sent such a lowly form of transport to carry her to Broomcott. She was unused to luxury at the convent. All she could contemplate was the exciting new life that awaited her at the Manor. She waved to the Sisters, their upturned faces now pale blurs in the failing light.

'Goodbye! Goodbye!'

'May God go with you, child,' Sister Ursula called softly.

'And remember your catechism!' Sister Joseph croaked. She shook her head as the wagon moved away. 'A hoyden if ever I saw one,' she muttered. 'The dear Lord only knows what will become of her with no good woman to shape her future!'

Abigail was silent as the wagon rumbled over the cobblestones of the market place. Presently they left the buildings behind and the wheels of the wagon bumped and thumped along the rutted lanes, passing only the occasional cottage. Jed glanced at her.

'I expect you be tired, Miss,' he speculated. 'A fair long way you've come today.'

Abigail gave him her brilliant smile. 'I felt tired in the coach. It was so stuffy, but not now. The air is so crisp and fresh here. I believe Broomcott is by the sea. I can't wait to see it.'

Jed smiled, captivated by the girl's lightness of spirit. 'We'd best go along by the coast road then. You'll get a good view of it, if it be not too dark by then. Have you not seen the sea before?'

'Oh yes—and sailed on it too,' Abigail told him proudly. 'Though not for a long time now. My papa was French, you see. I used to go and stay with him every summer. But now he is dead—in the revolution.'

Jed looked at her sympathetically. Poor child. He had heard terrifying tales of the dark deeds done in the revolution across the sea in France. His master, Thomas Hargreaves, had connections on the other side of the channel, he knew, but, although he was bailiff to the old man he was not in his confidence. Indeed he often wondered if old Thomas confided in anyone. Even his right hand seemed ignorant of the workings of his left!

'You'll have been to school at the convent, no doubt,' he remarked, thinking to divert the girl's attention from her father's sad end.

She nodded. 'Until a year and a half ago.

Then Papa could send no more money to the Sisters, so I worked with them instead, helping the poor and the sick and caring for the little orphan children.' She smiled, the dimple in her cheek twinkling merrily. 'It was much nicer than being in the schoolroom all day.'

The wagon rumbled on, the track winding over a hill and it was from the top of this that Abigail got her first sight of the village as it lay below. To her left a group of tall stones stood, silent and eerie in the half light. She pointed.

'What are those?'

Jed followed her gaze, 'They be the Dancin' Maids, Miss. In days gone by the village folk used to hold their May revels up here on this hill till in Puritan times they was forbidden. 'Tis said that a band of maids came up here at dawn one May day to dance and make merry, but as the sun came up they was turned to stone for their wickedness.'

Abigail shivered, thinking of the maids and their forbidden pleasures. What would it feel like, she wondered, to be turned to stone?

The salt breeze from the sea at last reached her nostrils and she threw back the hood of her cloak to let the wind blow through her hair, tied up behind in the bunch of unruly curls that Sister Joseph was wont to call 'That worldly mop'. But to Abigail's disappointment she could not see the sea, only hear it. It was by now too dark, and the cliffs being so high, the sea itself was far below them.

9

Jed stopped the horse for a moment to light a lantern, although he assured Abigail that they would soon be at Broomcott and that anyway, old Robin the horse would have known his way there blindfold.

She stared into the misty darkness, breathing the tangy damp air. Somewhere out there was France—home. Or was it home any more? She didn't really know where she belonged. Perhaps she would come in time to think of Broomcott as her home. She hoped so.

'Is Broomcott a nice place to live?' she asked wistfully 'Are the people there happy?'

Jed glanced at her ruefully. He'd better be careful what he said to the girl. After all, she was the old man's niece. 'They be as happy as most country folk, I suppose,' he said warily.

She looked at him. 'Are there a good many poor? I shall be able to help my uncle there,' she said enthusiastically. 'The Sisters taught me well in the care of the poor. I can brew herb medicines and make calf's-foot jelly. Uncle Thomas has no wife or daughter to do his sick visiting for him, has he?'

Jed could hardly suppress a laugh. Sick visiting indeed! Old Thomas Hargreaves had no sympathy with the sick, or anyone else unable to work. 'Parasites', he called them and would sooner speed their despatch than feed them! But he had not the heart to enlighten the girl on this fact. She would no doubt find out soon enough.

'No,' he said briefly. 'He has no wife or daughter.' He ran a hand thoughtfully over his stubbly chin as he looked again at the handsome girl beside him. She had spirit, that was sure. Would old Thomas break that spirit, he wondered. Somehow he thought not. This girl was no swooning wobbler for all she was gentle-born. There was something strong about her even though she looked so small and frail. He smiled to himself, looking forward to watching the reactions of uncle and niece to each other.

By the time they reached Broomcott Manor it was too dark for Abigail to see either the house or its surroundings. All she knew was that they crossed a field to reach it and came to a halt in a walled yard. Jed helped her down from the wagon.

'Welcome to Broomcott Manor, Miss. I'd best take you straight to the kitchen, if you don't mind,' he said. 'Sarah will've kept you a bit o' supper and I can get the skip-jack to give me a hand with the boxes.'

Abigail followed him into the kitchen, a large room with a stone-flagged floor, lit by the glowing coals on the wide hearth and the rush dips which stood on the table. A middle-aged woman and a young girl were employing the light of these to mend linen and they looked up as Abigail was introduced to them by Jed:

'Sarah—Bess—this is Miss Abigail Labeque,

11

the master's niece from over Salisbury way. Be there some supper for her, Sarah? I'll lay she'm hungry as a hunter!'

Sarah, the middle-aged housekeeper, got up reluctantly from the table giving Abigail a resentful, sour look. Another mouth to cook for—and fancy tastes if she was any judge. As if she didn't have enough to do and her with a bad leg too! Bess, the young maid-of-all-work, smiled shyly at Abigail, eyeing her fine wool travelling cloak with envy. It'd be nice to have a young lady in the house—someone of her own age. Lord knew it was dull enough here.

'Wake up you lazy-bones! I've work for 'ee!' Jed bent to shake the shoulder of someone asleep in the corner on a pile of sacks and Abigail saw that it was a scrawny small boy of about eight years old. He sat up, rubbing the sleep from his eyes and Jed hauled him to his feet by his collar. As they went out of the door he turned to Bess who still sat dreaming over her mending.

'Best go and tell the master Miss Abigail's here,' he said. 'I expect he'll want to see her.'

The girl got up without a word and, with a small courteous bob in Abigail's direction, left the room, taking one of the rush lights with her. Left alone with Sarah, Abigail took off her cloak and smiled at the older woman.

'I hope I don't cause you trouble. May I help?'

'Aye—that you may.' The woman looked at

12

her coldly. 'And I hope you aren't expectin' fancy livin' for you won't find it here! The master likes plain livin'.' She slapped a wooden trencher down on the table and began to spoon stew on to it from a dish she took from the brick oven at the side of the fireplace. She nodded her head towards a table by the wall. 'You'll find eatin' irons over there. Do you want beer?'

'Thank you.' Somewhat taken aback Abigail found the cutlery box and helped herself to a knife and a two-pronged fork both in a far from clean condition. She sat at the table and looked again at Sarah. 'You need have no fear, I am not accustomed to luxury,' she said. 'At the convent we lived very simply.'

'Convent—huh!' The woman banged a mug and a pitcher of beer down on the table, making it abundantly clear what she thought of such establishments.

Abigail found the mutton stew greasy and slightly rancid but she was so hungry that she ate it ravenously. She had just swallowed the last mouthful when Bess returned.

'The master says you're to come now,' she said, holding the door open for Abigail to pass. As she closed it she gave a shy smile. 'You mustn't mind Sarah, Miss. She be always cross. She'm got a bad leg and it pains her.'

Abigail smiled back. 'I would have like to wash and tidy myself before I was presented to my uncle,' she said. 'I feel so distrait.'

13

But the girl shook her head. 'He won't notice nuthin' like that, Miss. I think you look very nice.'

They went up a short flight of steps into a wide stone-flagged hall from which a heavily carved oak staircase went up. Bess put her hand on the door at the foot of it.

'In here, if you please, Miss.'

It was dark in the oak-panelled room, the only light coming from a single candle in a brass candlestick. It stood on a table at which sat an old man, poring over some papers, a quill in his hand. He was bald except for a fringe of grey hair round the back of his head. On the table before him stood a wooden stand bearing a pig-tail wig which he had obviously recently removed. One of his booted legs rested on a stool under the table and next to this lay a huge dog which lifted its head and growled menacingly as they entered. Thomas Hargreaves did not look up and Bess cleared her throat.

'A—hem. Miss Abigail, sir—if you please.'

Then he put down his quill and looked at her, Abigail saw to her disappointment that her uncle was not the rosy-faced country gentleman of her imaginings at all. Far from it. He had a lean, grey, pinched face with a hooked nose and his eyes were close together, small and mean as he squinted through the gloom at her.

'Come over here, girl!' he commanded,

14

then, to Bess: 'Get out, creature! Can't you see that I wish to become acquainted with my niece?'

Bess left them abruptly, closing the door behind her and Abigail was left alone with her uncle.

'Well—step up here, girl, where I can see you!' His voice was cracked and rough and his tone that which he would use to his horse. 'I trust they've not brought you up to be a niminy-piminy at that nunnery place. What's the matter—are you afraid of men, girl?'

Abigail stepped into the circle of light made by the candle and her small pointed chin lifted defiantly. 'I hope I am afraid of nothing sir,' she said in a clear voice.

The small black eyes darted over her. 'Hoity-toity! You're very pert, Miss! I hope you'll prove suitably grateful to me for my charity to you. I'll make no secret of it. I never got on with your mother's family and when she went off and married that Frenchman—ah well—' He trailed off. Something in the girl's eye made him check his words. He pursed his lips. 'Things do not prosper as they should here at Broomcott,' he said. 'I am not a wealthy man, so I shall expect you to earn your keep. There is plenty to do around the house.'

'I do not expect charity, sir,' Abigail told him. 'I shall be glad to work as best I can. I am very good with the sick—and with children. I could—'

But he gave a bark of derision. 'Sick! There are no sick here, girl. There is good country air in Broomcott and besides, I don't encourage sickness. No, you'll find plenty to do around the house. Sarah could do with bringing into line.' He waved his gnarled hand dismissively. 'Away with you now, girl. And tell that slut to come and get these boots off me. My gouty leg's as stiff as a post!' As Abigail reached the door he called out to her: 'I shall expect you to preside at my breakfast table at seven—and don't be late, girl, for I won't tolerate it!'

Abigail's room was at the back of the house, at the end of along, dark corridor. It was sparsely furnished and the bed with its great oak tester was hard and uncomfortable. She lay in the darkness staring at the sliver of new moon through the small mullioned window and in spite of her determination a tear slipped down her cheek. When she had heard that she was to come and share her uncle's home at Broomcott Manor she had envisaged a comfortable country house and a kind old gentleman, not this dreary, cold building full of unwelcoming people. She had never felt so alone in her life and suddenly she knew how the waifs and strays cared for by the nuns at St. Dominic's felt. The memory of the emptiness in their small faces filled her heart and she was swamped in despair. If only she could have stayed with them. Was she never to know love or kindness again?

Turning her head into the pillow she tried to stifle her sobs but it seemed that once she had given in to her tears a flood-gate was opened.

She didn't hear the handle turn or the door open, but her eyelids flew open as a light played on them.

'Don't 'ee cry like that, Miss.' Bess stood holding the rush light aloft and looking down at the weeping Abigail. Her feet were bare, the toes blue under the coarse calico night gown. 'Don't 'ee mind about Sarah. Her bark be worse than her bite,' she whispered. 'And as for your uncle, he be out most o' the time.'

Abigail swallowed hard, smiling up gratefully into the homely young face. 'Will you stay with me, Bess?' she begged. 'I hardly ever cry, but tonight I feel so lonely.'

'I know how you feels, Miss,' Bess said compassionately. 'I was mortal homesick when I first came to the Manor. I cried all night for my brothers and sisters—but stay with you—I dunno.'

'Oh, please, Bess—please.' The large brown eyes looked pleadingly up into hers and Bess hesitated no longer. Slipping into bed beside Abigail she covered her shoulders maternally as she had done so often with her young brothers and sisters, murmuring soothingly to her: 'There, I won't leave you. Go to sleep now, do.'

Abigail sighed. 'My uncle says that I am to work in the house and bring Sarah into line,' she said. 'I'm afraid she will resent me fearfully. Will you be my friend, Bess?'

Bess shook her head doubtfully. 'I don't think that be right, Miss. Not if you be going to be mistress here.' She giggled. 'It'd serve Sarah right though. She'm had her own way long enough!'

Abigail looked into Bess's eyes in the light from the moon. 'But I shall *need* a friend. It's not that I don't know how to run a household. We were taught that at the convent. But when I think of Sarah's face! Like a thunder cloud!'

Bess giggled again, stuffing the bedclothes into her mouth in case she might be heard. 'You'll have to show her you'm the Mistress right enough. Oh, I'm going to *enjoy* watching that!'

'I can do it if you promise to be my friend—oh, say you will—*dearest* Bess,' Abigail pleaded.

Bess flushed with pleasure in the darkness. No one had ever called her 'dearest' before. Miss Abigail would make a grand friend and no mistake. She was so pretty and she smelled so good.

'Well—' she said slowly. 'If I do it will have to be a secret mind.'

Abigail hugged her. 'Of course, anything you say. I promise'.

They lay warmly together in the darkness for a while till Bess suddenly said: 'Listen—you can hear the sea from here.'

Abigail listened and sure enough she heard the distant thud and roar of the waves on the shore. Her arms tightened round the servant girl. 'Will you show it to me tomorrow?' She asked. 'Oh, I love the sea!'

Bess nodded. 'I will. I'll show you everything. Maybe I'll tell you my secret too—when I get to know you better.'

She smiled and wriggled into a more comfortable position. 'It be a prime secret and no one else knows!'

Abigail's eyes closed, the lids as heavy as lead. Perhaps life here at Broomcott wouldn't be so bad after all. She wanted to coax Bess's secret out of her there and then and her lips started to frame the words, but somehow they were never spoken. The sleep she had thought would never come claimed her at last, with the sound of the sea for a lullaby.

CHAPTER TWO

Broomcott Manor looked no better in daylight than it had in the dark. Built in the previous century of stout Portland stone it sat, grey and solid, enclosed in its own grounds by a high stone wall; its roof mossy and its chimneys straight and tall. It would have been a handsome house if it had not been for its sad air of neglect. Dust and cobwebs lay thick in every cranny; where there were carpets they were threadbare and filthy and as for the domestic regions, they were a disgrace. To Abigail's disgust, she found pigs rooting in the dairy while hens pecked among the rubbish on the buttery floor. She was appalled, but at least it gave her something with which to unbraid the formidable Sarah.

Her uncle had given her free rein and since the first morning when she had appeared in the kitchen wearing a serviceable grey frock and apron, a white muslin cap covering her hair, she had made her presence felt. Though it took all the skill and courage she possessed she was determined to show her uncle that she was no parasite to live on his charity.

The Manor House had been cleaned thoroughly from top to bottom till it shone like a new pin and, that accomplished, Abigail took upon herself the task of teaching Sarah how to prepare an edible meal. At first the woman was hostile and rebellious, but at last she could not deny that the master's niece knew what she was about and although she would have admitted it to no one she felt a grudging admiration for Abigail who had not merely ordered her uncle's servants to do the work, but had rolled up her sleeves and worked with them till her slim white hands were as rough and blistered as their own.

One of Abigail's greatest admirers was Jed Harker, the bailiff. He wouldn't have believed a slip of a girl could have wrought such a change in the place and he was gratified to have his first impression of her confirmed. Miss Abigail would set things buzzing and no mistake. Not that she got any thanks from her uncle. Thomas Hargreaves had said nothing to his niece or to anyone else, but secretly he congratulated himself on getting a free housekeeper of such merit.

Jed had been helping Abigail with the garden that lay to the west side of the house. Once it had been beautiful, its high stone walls mellow with age and giving shelter from the sea winds to the flowers and shrubs that grew there. Once they had cleared the mass of weeds and undergrowth Abigail found to her delight, roses, hollyhocks and delphiniums, also a small herb garden which she set about re-cultivating at once. She found mint, parsley and thyme which she hoped Sarah would make use of in the kitchen. And rosemary, lavender and verbena with which she would make a *potpourri* to make the linen fragrant.

As they worked she and Jed chatted. She asked him questions and he told her a little about the unrest in the village and the reason why her uncle was so unpopular.

'He has plans to enclose the land, Miss. Leastways, that's what the village folk think and I believe they're right.'

Abigail frowned. 'Enclose it? What does that mean?'

21

He straightened his back and looked at her. 'Well, Miss, at the moment the village folk are tenants. They have their strips and they tend them and pay their rents and tithes. Your uncle wants to put fences round whole plots—do away wi' the strips, if you get my meanin.'

'But what about the land that has to be left fallow?' Abigail asked intelligently. 'If a whole field is to be left fallow won't that be very wasteful?'

The bailiff shook his head. 'Turnips can be grown on fallow land now, Miss. 'Tis the modern way and 'tis called 'rotation'. But anyway, Mr. Hargreaves be thinkin' of turnin' most of the land over to sheep and if he does that there'll be work for no more'n a few o' the village folk.'

Abigail was silent. What Jed was telling her explained the hostility she had sensed among the people of Broomcott. Last week when Bess had taken her to visit her family there had been some talk of their losing their common grazing rights. At the time she hadn't properly understood but now it was becoming clear.

'The common land,' she said thoughtfully to Jed. 'Surely the villagers will still have that?'

But he shook his head. 'By the law o' the land that belongs to the Squire too,' he said. 'And though I wouldn't put it round it be my belief that Mr. Hargreaves means to enclose that too.'

Abigail said nothing. It was not seemly to

22

discuss her uncle's affairs with a servant, but what she had heard troubled her greatly. If these people did not have their plots of land and their few animals how would they live and feed their families? It was true that some of the women had looms and wove sailcloth and sacking; a few were skilled in the craft of glovemaking too, but what they earned at that would not support them. She determined to talk to her uncle about it as soon as an opportunity arose. She was deep in these thoughts when suddenly something that Jed was saying caught her attention:

'If Mr. Philip was to come home he wouldn't see the village folk go down. That I do know!'

She turned to him. 'Who is Mr. Philip?'

He looked at her in surprise. 'Why, the master's stepson. I thought you'd know, being kin. He were already a grown lad when the master married his mother and they never got on. When his mother died he went away to London and now he hardly ever comes to Broomcott. Can't say I blames him though.' Jed chuckled. 'For the gentry it's gamin', wine and women all the time, so they do say.' He bit his lip. 'Oh—if you'll beg pardon, Miss.'

'It's quite all right, Jed. ' Abigail tossed her head. 'So that was all he thought about, this Philip. In that case Broomcott was better off without him!'

But if Abigail wondered why she had heard

nothing of her uncle's stepson before the matter was soon to be righted. It was that very evening at dinner that Thomas Hargreaves first mentioned Philip Jefferson.

After his second helping of boiled mutton with caper sauce he pushed back his chair, wiping his chin with a snowy napkin and eyeing his great-niece with guarded satisfaction. She had proved more useful than he had ever dared to hope, transforming his home from the pigsty it had become to a place of modest grace and comfort. He had not known such a civilized existence since the death of his second wife ten years ago.

As she sat there in the candlelight in her blue taffeta dress, the frothy lace of the fichu at her breast enhanced the creaminess of her skin. The firelight made the chestnut lights dance in her brown hair and old Thomas drew in his mouth shrewdly. It was obvious that a girl like that would not be with him long. Soon she would be spoken for in marriage. He had seen that odious son of the parson's casting sheep's eyes at her in church last Sunday. But what to do about it—unless—. Suddenly a brilliant idea came to him; so brilliant that at first it took his breath away, rendering him incapable of speech. Philip Jefferson, his late wife's son by a previous marriage, had been left money by his mother. He was to receive it only when he married or reached the age of thirty, whichever came first. Also, he would only receive it if the marriage was approved by his stepfather. Why, then, should the boy not marry Abigail? Thomas knew that he would like to get his hands on the money. If he took to the girl he might stay at Broomcott and take over the running of the estate, leaving Thomas free for other business he had lately become involved in. If not he could return to his doubtless debauched life in London, leaving Abigail here to keep house for him at the Manor.

He glanced at Abigail and cleared his throat. 'I have been meaning to speak to you, child.'

Abigail looked up from her embroidery. 'What is it, Uncle? Was the mutton not to your liking?'

Thomas shook his head. 'It was passable—a little overspiced, but no matter—' He did not believe in paying women compliments. It made them uppish. Again he cleared his throat. 'It was something else I wished to tell you. I have chosen a husband for you, girl. It's high time you were wed.'

The embroidery dropped into her lap as she stared at him in dismay. 'Oh! But I had thought when the time came—to choose for myself.'

The old man gave a short bark of mirthless laughter. 'Hah! Is that the nonsense they stuffed your head with at the nunnery? What a notion! Who would you choose, I wonder, if it were left to you? No. I have the perfect husband for yon—my own stepson, Philip Jefferson.'

Abigail swallowed hard. 'But, sir—we are not even acquainted—and anyway—I thought I had been of some small service to you here. Do you now wish me to leave?'

Thomas shook his head. 'On the contrary. I hope that you will make your home here. The Manor will pass to Philip on my death anyway, as I have no heir. As for being acquainted, that will be remedied as soon as I write and bid Philip to come and be presented to you.'

But Abigail bit her lip, her cheeks reddening with her growing annoyance. 'And if we do not suit each other, sir—what then?'

Thomas's patience snapped and he leaned forward, glaring at Abigail ferociously with his beady black eyes. 'Listen to me, Miss,' he said, his voice harsh and grating. 'When you were cast upon my mercy there was no money for your keep. There will be no dowry for you when you wed either. You are lucky to have been offered such a match. My stepson will come into a considerable fortune on his marriage. The boy has no taste in women so I am to approve his choice. He will agree to take you without question—that or lose his fortune. I shall write to him tonight. You may consider yourself betrothed!'

Abigail jumped to her feet, the embroidery falling unheeded on to the hearth. 'No money?

But in the letter Mother Angela received it said that there was money for me in a bank in Winchester. It was to be mine when I married!'

'That money was all gone by the time your father died,' Thomas told her. 'He had run into financial difficulties owing to the revolution, as you are no doubt aware. The money had to be made available to the convent and was all used up for your keep during your stay there. So you see, child, you are dependent entirely on my good nature. You will do as you are told!'

* * *

What is Philip Jefferson like? Does he come often to the Manor?' Abigail looked up from the kitchen table where she, Sarah and Bess were busy washing eggs. She had lain awake all night thinking of her uncle's proposal. She saw through his reasoning quite clearly. The match would be to his advantage, however it turned out. But think as she may, she could see no way to avoid it without becoming destitute.

Sarah looked up at her mistress and grinned smugly to herself. She had been about to enter the room and clear the dinner table last night when Thomas Hargreaves's words had reached her and she had spent ten minutes with her ear firmly pressed to the keyhole. 'Mr. Philip?' she said. 'He don't come 'ere often. If you asks me he be 'avin' too good a time in

27

London. More often drunk than sober, so I've 'eard tell. Gamblin' half the night and cavortin' with lewd women. A rare old life *he* lead.'

Bess's eyes were like saucers. 'What are lewd women, Sarah?'

Sarah boxed her ears. 'Never you mind— just get on with your work.' She glanced at Abigail. 'I'm sure *you* wouldn't like him, Miss. Oh, no, he wouldn't be to *your* liking at all!' Inwardly she glowed with satisfaction. *That* would give Miss Bossy-boots something to think about!

Later that afternoon Abigail and Bess sat together in their favourite spot on the clifftop almost hidden by the tall wiry grass and the clumps of sea-pinks. Abigail was silent, gazing down at the surf as it gently frothed against the rocks below, while Bess chattered on in her customary way.

'What I can't understand, Miss Abi, is how you come to be so good at lookin' after a house—cookin' an' that. I thought that them schools for young ladies only taught music an' dancin' an' the like.'

Abigail smiled and shook her head. 'They do teach those things, of course, but they also teach the practical crafts. Besides, for the past year and a half I have spent all my time helping the Sisters at their work, both in and out of the convent.'

Bess gazed at her with admiration. 'I do

think you'm clever, Miss Abi.' She edged closer. 'Sarah do say that the master've got 'is eye on you for Mr. Philip. Be that true?'

Abigail sighed. 'I'm afraid it is, Bess, though I'll not give way to it if I can think of a way out!'

Bess's eyes were round. 'They do say as Mr. Philip be 'andsome as they come. Wouldn't you like to be mistress o' the Manor then?'

'I want to *live*!' Abigail said vehemently, sitting up and throwing a stone down to bounce over the jagged rocks. 'I want to know what it is to have adventure and excitement. I want to love the man I marry!'

Bess giggled. 'Oh , Miss Abi, you do ask for a lot! I think 'tis only the men that 'as excitement—soldiers and such. The women has to bide at home and have the babies.'

Abigail made no reply but sat tugging at the tough grass. Bess ran her tongue over her lips.

'I do know what you mean about about love though,' she said shyly. 'I told you I had a secret well that be it—I love somebody.'

Abigail looked at her delightedly, her face brightening. 'Do you really, Bess? Who is he— do tell me?'

The girl blushed. 'Oh—it be no one you know, Miss. His namc's Jack. It has to be a secret 'cos my Pa don't like 'im and wouldn't never let us be wed.'

'Oh, but why?' Abigail asked.

'On account of 'ow his mother wasn't never

29

married,' Bess replied. 'Some do say Jack's pa was a tinker—some a middle-man. My Jack don't work the land either, like my pa. He fishes with a man who has a boat further down the coast at Mortstone.'

Abigail frowned. 'What is wrong with fishing? It's an honest living. And poor Jack can't help the circumstances of his birth.'

Bess nodded eagerly. 'That's what I do say—but Pa, he beat me when I said it to him. Said I wasn't to see Jack again. He don't trust fishermen, you see.' She lowered her voice although there was clearly no one to hear— 'There's a lot of smugglin' goes off round 'ere.'

Abigail felt her blood tingle. 'And is Jack a smuggler. Go on, Bess, you can tell me.'

'No, 'e baint!' Bess said hotly. She bit her lip and glanced sideways at Abigail. 'He *don't* smuggle. He promised me it weren't that but he do something with the boat that do earn him extra money and when he'm got enough we'm going to run away together!' She sat up, her cheeks scarlet. 'There—I've told you all now.'

Abigail's eyes were alight. 'What *does* he do, Bess? You must know. I promise you I won't tell a soul if you tell me.'

'I can't tell you, Miss Abi, for I don't rightly know myself. All I knows is that when Jack goes out on one o' his night jaunts I slips out to meet him. 'Tis the only chance I get to see him. But what they do—'im an' the others, he won't tell me. He says it's best I don't know.'

Abigail's heart was racing with excitement. 'You mean you sneak out at night when everyone is asleep—to meet your lover? Oh Bess, how romantic! What do you say to each other? What do you do?'

Bess blushed and lowered her eyes. 'Nuthin much—there don't never be time. But Jack do say he loves me and we—we—kiss.'

Abigail clasped her hands together in delight. 'Oh, Bess, you are lucky. To have someone of your own—to love and *be* loved. Tell me, where do you meet?'

'At the bottom of the cliff path—' Bess pointed. 'There's a little cave. It's where they do hide the boat while they goes off to the Dolphin Inn. I usually meets Jack there.'

'And you said women don't have adventures!' Abigail exclaimed. 'When all the time you're having the greatest adventures yourself! Oh, do show me the path, Bess. And the cave where you meet.'

Bess put a hand on her arm. 'Oh, Miss Abp—you won't let on to no one, will you? My pa'd kill me if 'e ever found out!'

A glint came into Abigail's eyes. 'Of course I won't if you'll promise me something.'

The girl looked at her fearfully. 'What—what be that, Miss Abi?'

'That you'll take me with you next time you go—oh, *please* Bess—just the once.'

Bess looked at her young mistress in horror.

31

The brown eyes were alight with flecks of golden fire. When Miss Abi looked like that there was no denying her anything. She gave up all hope of refusing. 'If I do you'll have to keep out o' sight,' she said waveringly. 'Jack made me promise not to tell a soul. I don't know what he'd say—'

Abigail jumped up, all her gloomy thoughts quite forgotten. 'But I'm not 'anyone' am I, Bess? And I promise you I'll keep your secret to my grave!' She held out her hand. 'Come—show me the path now! And as we go you can tell me what Jack is like. I want to know every detail!'

The path was steep and winding and Bess warned her repeatedly to beware of the loose stones. 'It be really slippy when it rains,' she said.

As they descended the roar of the sea grew louder and at last they came out from behind some tall rocks at the foot of the cliff to find the waves only a few yards away, throwing spray into their faces. Abigail took a deep breath and spread her arms wide.

'Oh, I love the sea!' She turned and pointed to a small hollow in the cliff. 'Is that the cave?'

Bess nodded. 'It's not deep but the tide never comes up this far except in rough weather. It's where they hides the boat.'

'Is he handsome, your Jack?' Abigail asked. 'Has he dark flashing eyes and curly hair? Is he strong and powerful?'

'Bless you no, Miss,' Bess giggled. 'Jack've got straight hair as yellow as the sand an' eyes to match. He baint all that tall either, though I'll lay he'm still growin'. He be only eighteen, y'see.' Seeing Abigail's disappointed expression she added loyally: 'He do be strong though—strong as a horse. An' I think he'm got a handsome face, even if some don't!'

Abigail hugged her. 'I'm sure he's quite beautiful! Well—when do we go, Bess?'

'I have to watch for the signal,' the girl chewed her lip, unwilling to disclose Jack's secret. 'There be an old dead tree atop o' the cliff. When Jack's goin' out he hangs a rag from one o' the branches. Then I knows to meet him.'

'And you won't forget to tell me when it is, will you, Bess?'

Bess shook her head. 'No, I won't, Miss. But only the once, mind.'

'Of course, Bess. Only the once.'

It was at breakfast time ten days later that Thomas Hargreaves told Abigail that he had had a communication from his stepson. Thomas's own letter, proclaiming that he had chosen a bride for Philip, had gone to London by hand with Jed Harker whom Thomas had sent to the capital on other business. He had brought the reply back with him on his return.

'Unfortunately he cannot visit us for some time,' Thomas explained tetchily. 'He says he has urgent business to attend to, though what that can be I have no idea. It seems his meeting with his future wife will have to wait.'

But Abigail hardly heard his words. It was a fine May morning and she had taken a walk almost as soon as the sun was up. The hedges and trees with their bright blossoms had been spangled with dew and merry with birdsong, but one tree wore the most exciting decoration of all.

The old dead oak pointed a ghostly, salt-bleached arm out to sea and as Abigail drew near to it her heart had quickened at what she had seen. From the stiff, grey branch a piece of white cloth fluttered in the wind. It was the signal Bess had spoken of—tonight she was to have her adventure!

CHAPTER THREE

'Was it a white rag or a coloured one?'

'White—I told you, *white!*' Abigail said impatiently.

The two girls worked together at the slab in the buttery. Sarah had gone for her afternoon rest and they were alone, each holding a pair of wooden 'pats' and shaping the golden mass from the churn. Bess was exasperatingly calm.

'White means they'll be going to the Dolphin tonight to get their orders,' she explained. 'A coloured rag means a 'cargo' be

34

due.'

'Do you go to meet Jack when he's to be at the Dolphin, then?' Abigail asked.

Bess nodded. 'If I can, though I don't often. It be too risky. Women baint welcome at the Dolphin, so if I goes I has to put on my brother's clothes and try not to be noticed.'

Abigail drew in her breath, her cheeks colouring. 'Could you get me some of your brother's clothes to wear?' she asked.

Bess stared at her in dismay. She was beginning to wish she had never told her young mistress of her meetings with Jack. 'You?' she gasped. 'You can't go to the Dolphin, Miss Abi!'

Abigail's eyes flashed. 'I can if you can! Besides, you promised.'

The girl shook her head vigorously. 'No! I said when I went to the *beach*. 'Tis too dangerous for you to go to the inn.'

Abigail's chin came out stubbornly. 'You go!'

'I know—but I can take care of myself.'

'If you can, so can I!'

Bess gave a sigh of resignation. 'Oh well— I'll see what I can do. There's another thing that makes it more dangerous going to the Dolphin—it's earlier. Your uncle an' Sarah might not be abed.'

But Abigail's eyes only twinkled the more with excitement 'All the more fun—!' she said.

She sent Bess scuttling off home for the

35

boy's clothing telling her to be back again before Sarah came down from her rest, and the girl got back with her bundle in the nick of time. She thrust the things at Abigail, her face flushed with the exertion of running across the Manor fields.

'There!' she said breathlessly. 'You'll be the death o' me, Miss Abi, that you will! I only just managed to get past our ma wi' them. An' mind you don't let anything happen to them, they be our Arthur's best!'

Up in her room Abigail tried the boy's clothes on—there was a stout pair of breeches, stockings and shoes, a coarse calico shirt and a jacket. And to top them all off and hide her hair, a woollen stocking cap. Pushing her hair up under this she regarded herself critically in the mirror. Yes, she was sure she would pass for a lad, especially if she rubbed some dirt on her face and hands. Her heart fluttered with excitement. She could hardly wait for it to be bedtime.

It seemed to Abigail that her uncle would never dispense with her company that evening. In spite of the fact that she refilled his tankard with ale more times than usual he seemed wide awake, even asking her to read to him from the news sheet that Jed had brought back from London with him. He lit his long clay pipe and leaned back in his chair to listen, his eyes half closed. At last, however, Sarah announced a late visitor and Abigail was able to escape.

In the dim hall she passed a stout gentleman whom she recognized as the Reverend Frederick Wilford, vicar of the parish church of St. Catherine which, though she had been brought up Catholic, her uncle made her attend each Sunday. She dropped him a grudging curtsey and hurried up the stairs.

She found Bess already in her room, quaking with nerves.

'Oh, Miss Abi—I been thinking. Do you think we should? What if we be caught—?'

But Abigail was not to be put off. 'Oh, stuff and rubbish! We won't be caught. Sarah always goes to sleep over the kitchen fire as you well know. We can creep out through the buttery while she sleeps and my uncle talks with the parson.'

And so, fifteen minutes later the two girls, dressed in their borrowed clothing, crept past the snoring cook and out of the house into the warm spring night. The tension over. Abigail looked at Bess and laughed aloud.

'You should see your face! You look like a frightened rabbit!'

Bess looked back at the grubby laughing face indignantly. 'Well! What about your'n? You looks like our Arthur after he'm been rattin'!'

The Dolphin was a low, thatched building on the coast road. It stood perched on top of the cliffs about a mile and a half out of the

37

village and was frequented, not by the menfolk of Broomcott as much as by the small community of fisherfolk whose cottages straggled along the coast road and down to Mortstone Cove a mile away.

In order to get in unnoticed the girls waited in the darkness outside till a group of men came along, then tagged on behind them, making their way straight to the shadowy area close to the huge fireplace and keeping well out of sight.

The room was crowded and smoky, the air thick with the odour of fish from the unwashed clothing of the fishermen, and Abigail, who loved fresh air, soon felt stifled. She looked at Bess impatiently.

'Well—can you see him?'

Bess shook her head, but a moment later the door opened to admit three men, two of them in their thirties or thereabouts and obviously fishermen, the third, a young, fresh-faced lad with tow-coloured hair. Bess clutched Abigail's arm.

'That be my Jack!'

'Go on then, aren't you going to speak to him?'

Abigail's voice had risen with her impatience and Bess coloured and pinched her hard. 'Keep your voice down, do! The other men'll go into the back room to meet their gaffer. Jack'll have a drink while he'm waitin' and he'll slip outside to meet me. When I see him go—I'll follow.'

'Oh,' Abigail said flatly. Now that the initial excitement was over she was finding it all rather dull. Then something surprising happened. The door opened again, and this time it admitted a familiar figure—one whom she had seen less than an hour ago. She clutched Bess's arm.

'Look, it's Mr. Wilford. I never thought to see him here!'

Bess nodded. 'He's supposed to have a special liking for the fishin' folk from Mortstone. Oh! Jack's going outside. I must go.' She got up and made for the door and a moment later Abigail found herself alone.

She waited half an hour. The men who had gone into the back room remained there and Bess and Jack did not reappear. Smoke from the wood fire and from the clay pipes of the customers made her eyes and throat smart and she longed to go outside. Surely Bess must be ready to go home now! Making up her mind, she rose and began to make her way towards the door, elbowing her way through the throng of male bodies, her head down to hide her face. Then suddenly there was a bump and she felt herself showered with ale. Looking up she saw to her horror that she had cannoned into Parson Wilford, spilling his mug of ale down his clothes as well as her own. He gave a hoarse cry and before she could escape he had caught her by the collar.

'Ho there, you young good-for-nothing! What do you mean by it, eh?'

'S—sorry, sir,' Abigail stammered, trying to make her voice deeper in tone.

The parson's ruddy face glared angrily into hers. 'Who are you, boy? What's your name?'

'A—Alfred—sir' Abigail's heart felt as though it might stop beating at any moment. The large ham-like hand still held her collar in an iron grip while the angry bloodshot eyes burned into hers intently. She felt sure that he knew she was not a boy and that he would recognize her.'

'Alfred?' He boomed. 'I know of no Alfred. Who is your father? I know I have seen you somewhere before and it cannot have been in my church!'

She was still holding her breath, her mind searching feverishly for a reply, when a rough-looking man touched the parson's sleeve and jerked his head towards a group of men sitting in a corner. Immediately the parson let go of Abigail's collar and turned away with a few words of warning.

With a sigh of relief, she made her way gratefully towards the door and, once outside, breathed deeply of the salt air. It was very dark and she peered around for Bess, not daring to call her name in case someone heard her. She was just wondering whether to make her way back to the Manor alone when the girl appeared at her side as though from nowhere.

'Here I be, Miss Abi. We'd best be gettin' back now.'

'Thank goodness. I thought you were never coming!' Abigail grabbed Bess's arm. 'I was almost caught in there. I knocked Parson Wilford's ale clear out of his hand. I thought I was done, I swear it! He called on my uncle tonight and we passed in the hall. I felt sure he recognized me!'

Bess gasped. 'Oh, Miss! I said you shouldn't o' come. Make haste now before your uncle finds you a'missin'.'

'What did Jack say?' Abigail asked as they hurried homewards. 'Is there to be a cargo soon?'

'Tomorrow night,' Bess whispered. 'But I don't think you should come. Jack were in a right pother when I told 'im I'd brought you along tonight. He said if the Eagle should get to hear—'

'The Eagle?' Abigail interrupted. 'Who is the Eagle?'

'He be the gaffer of them all,' Bess explained. 'No one knows his real name or the names of any o' them that plans it all. They reckons that way no one can't give the game away.'

Abigail's interest rekindled sharply. 'I'm coming with you to the beach tomorrow night,' she said decisively. 'Oh, Bess, I've *got* to! I'll stay out of sight, I promise—and you needn't tell Jack I'm there.'

Bess shook her head vigorously, her face creased with anxiety. '*No*, Miss Abi! It's no good you plaguin' me, I just *can't* take you. It's more'n I dare do. Besides,' she added lamely, 'our Arthur'll be wantin 'is clothes back.'

But the following night saw the two girls slipping out of the Manor once more. Once Abigail made up her mind upon a thing there was no stopping her, as Bess was fast discovering. Tonight it was easier. The time given for the arrival of the 'cargo' was midnight and everyone else in the house had been asleep for some time when they tiptoed down the back stairs and out into the night.

Although there was a full moon it was not as clear as the previous night. A chill mist drifting in from the sea obscured the moon's light and from time to time they were plunged into inky blackness. It was dry, however and the cliff path was not too difficult to negotiate. Bess, being used to it, went first, looking over her shoulder occasionally to see how her mistress was faring. She was wishing with all her heart that she had never confided in Miss Abigail. She was so headstrong and determined. She would surely get them both into trouble before they were done; Jack too, most likely. This secret work he did was certainly against the law, that much she was sure of, and if he were to be caught because of her, she would never forgive herself. Miss Abi saw it all as a sort of game. That, she told herself, was the gentry all

42

over! At last they reached the foot of the path and stood amidst the shelter of the tall rocks. Bess stopped, holding up her hand and placing a finger against her lips.

'We'll wait here,' she whispered. 'Till we sees the boat come. When they'm beached it the men go off to make sure the coast be clear. That's when Jack be free to meet me. You stay here and remember—*keep out of sight.*'

Abigail shivered, half with cold from the damp, chill air and half with a delicious thrill of excitement. The mist hung like a blanket over the surface of the water and the sea was calm, only a slight swell moving it. The two stood perfectly still, listening to the gentle breaking of the waves and the rattle of the shingle at the water's edge. Then presently they heard another sound: muffled voices and the creak of oars. Bess grasped Abigail's arm and pointed as a dim shape began to emerge from the mist. In the boat, Abigail just made out three figures. Bess held a finger to her lips.

'Remember what you promised—keep out of sight.'

Abigail nodded and watched, her heart beating rapidly as the outline of the boat and its occupants grew clearer. She heard the hull scrape against the shingle as two of the figures leapt out and began to drag the small craft up the beach. The third man, who wore a heavy cloak, stepped out and helped them the last few yards into the shelter of the cave, then, the three went off in different directions.

The girls looked at each other. 'I be going to meet Jack now,' Bess said hesitantly. 'It'd be best if you went back.'

Abigail bit her lip, disappointed. 'Is that all? Is there nothing else for Jack to do?'

Bess shook her head. 'No. His part is done when they lands. He's supposed to go home— 'cos he baint allowed to know what happens to the 'cargo'. But he waits for me in a secret place instead.' She looked at Abigail uncertainly. 'You will go straight back to the Manor, now, won't you, Miss Abi?'

Abigail lowered her lashes and nodded obediently. She had no intention of going back to the Manor when the excitement was only just beginning but she gave Bess a little push. 'Go and meet your precious Jack. I'll go—and I'll be careful. I promise.'

She watched as the girl set off over the sands, keeping to the shadows at the bottom of the cliff, then, as she disappeared behind a rock all was silent again except for the rhythmic lapping of the waves on the shore. Abigail shivered and pulled the woolly cap closer round her face. She must see what was in the boat. Just one peep before she began to make her way back. She simply couldn't turn and go tamely home without knowing what the mysterious 'cargo' consisted of, although she already had a good idea. True, Jack had sworn to Bess that he was not engaged in smuggling,

44

yet it seemed clear that he was. What else would involve the secret landing of a boat at the dead of night in a deserted cove: Bess merely believed the lad because she loved him and chose to think him innocent.

When she was certain that the cove was empty she crept out into the moonlight. The cave was about a dozen yards from the cliff path and she tiptoed stealthily towards it, keeping to the shadows in case anyone should be keeping watch from above. At the mouth of the cave she paused. The boat was pulled well up into the hollow but she could see a mound in the stern, covered now by the cloak the third man had worn. It was quite a small mound and for a moment or two she stood, speculating as to what it could be. It seemed so little for three men and a lad to have risked their lives for. Brandy, tea, silk? Which, she wondered. Certainly not all three.

Creeping up to thc boat she carefully lifted a corner of the cloak, but dropped it again and stepped back in alarm as there was a small sound and a movement beneath. What was it? An animal of some sort? Consumed with curiosity she stepped forward and lifted the cloak again and as the moon moved from behind a cloud in its full brilliance she saw what the 'cargo' was. Two small children lay in the boat's stern on a pile of sacks, asleep in each other's arms. Her heart contracted with pity. Where had they come from? And where were their parents? But before she could begin to think of the answer to these questions she was startled by a cry behind her and a man's voice calling:

'Ho there! Who are you? What do you want?'

She spun round, her eyes wide with fear, to see a tall powerfully built man standing in the mouth of the cave, his feet apart and his hands on his hips. As he made to move towards her she made a quick dart, ducked under this arm as he made to grab her and set off as fast as she could towards the cliff path. As she ran she stumbled among the rocks and sand. Arthur's shoes were several sizes too large for her and as she began to ascend the steep path the loose stones slipped and slid beneath her feet, making her progress almost impossible.

She heard the man's feet pounding after her and her heart was a hot, throbbing lump in her throat. Clawing with her hands at the wiry grass at the path's edge, she scrambled on upwards, half running, half crawling. But she had only gone a few yards by this method when a clump of grass came away in her hand and she staggered backwards. Strong hands grasped at her ankles and she fell with a cry, slithering to a stop at the man's feet with a bump that almost threw him off balance too.

Grabbing her by the shoulders he heaved her to her feet and shook her till she was dizzy.

'*Now*—Who are you? What is your name?

Who sent you?' he demanded sternly, his dark eyes glaring down at her angrily.

Incapable of speech, she stared at him open-mouthed.

'Let's have a proper look at you!' The man grabbed her by the collar and jerked her round till the light of the moon fell on her face. As he did so, the woollen stocking cap fell to the ground and Abigail's thick dark curls cascaded down her back. The man gave a surprised cry and relaxed his rough hold on her.

'God in Heaven! By all that's holy—a *girl*!'

Abigail thrust her chin out. '*Woman*, sir—if you don't mind!'

For a second they stared at each other in a stunned silence, then a thin wail from the direction of the cave made them turn, startling them both into action. Forgetting how afraid she had been, Abigail broke free of the man's grasp and ran back across the sand to the cave, her only thought for the crying, frightened children. She knew that the man was hot on her heels but she didn't care now. Her one thought was to keep him from harming the children.

When she reached the cave, the little boy, who could not have been more than three years old, was standing up in the boat, looking round him, his eyes wide with fear and his mouth crumpled. Abigail lifted him out and gathered him to her.

'There, poppet. Don't cry. You're quite safe.

I won't let anyone hurt you.'

The little boy stopped crying and gazed into her eyes.

'*Ou est ma mère?*' he asked pitifully.

Abigail stared at him and then at the man who stood in the mouth of the cave. 'He's French!' she said in surprise.

He nodded and she turned her attention again to the child and to his sister who had now also wakened and sat up in the boat demanding—in French—to know where she was.

Abigail comforted them both, speaking to them soothingly in their native tongue and persuading them to lie down and go back to sleep while she covered them warmly with the cloak. At last she turned to the man.

'Whose children are they?' she demanded angrily. 'They need a woman's care. Where are you taking them?'

He came into the cave and peered at her closely. 'Where did you learn to speak French like that?' he asked.

She shrugged impatiently. 'My father is French—' she bit her lip. 'I should say—*was*—he is dead now.'

His expression softened. 'In the Terror?'

She nodded. 'Yes, My name is—' But he stepped close to her, holding up his hand.

'No! Do not tell me your name, Mademoiselle. We none of us use our names and I shall not tell you mine. Tell me this

48

though: What are you doing here at this hour? A young lady of breeding should be in her bed at this time of night!'

She looked at him now properly for the first time and saw that he was younger than she had at first thought. As well as being tall and broad-shouldered he was good to look at. His eyes were fine and dark and he wore his own hair tied back simply. His clothes were austere, though well cut, and there was something about his speech and manner that told her he was well-educated and of good breeding. Suddenly she felt foolish. A silly girl, out on a moonlight jaunt.

'I—I have not been long at Broomcott, sir,' she began. 'I find life tedious here and I had heard of some excitement that was to take place here tonight. I came to see what was afoot.'

His brow clouded. 'From where did you hear this? Who has been talking?'

'From my maid, sir.' She did not wish to make trouble for Bess and her beloved Jack, but the look on the young man's face made her want to reassure him that he was not betrayed. 'Jack, the lad who was with you, is her sweetheart,' she added hurriedly. 'She will certainly tell no one as it is the only chance they get to meet and she knows nothing of your 'cargos', that I do know.'

'How can you be so positive of that?' he asked, his eyes searching hers.

In spite of herself a smile lifted the corners of her mouth. 'Because, sir, if she had known I would certainly have wrung the secret from her. You can assure yourself of that!'

His eyebrows lifted, then he laughed softly. 'I can well believe it, Mademoiselle! And so, in order to partake of a little adventure, you dressed up in these unbecoming clothes and crept out to the beach. Are you now satisfied?'

Abigail blushed, aware for the first time of her dirty face and dishevelled appearance. She lifted her head defiantly. 'No, sir. I am not satisfied!' She glanced again in the direction of the boat, while they had been talking she had worked out her own idea of who the children were and what they were doing here. She stepped closer to the man, lowering her voice. 'I believe you are helping the people of my father's poor country in some way and I—I would like to be allowed to help you—for his sake.'

He stared at her, his eyes widening. 'Bravely spoken, *ma petite*. But I could not allow it.' He turned away and sat on a flat rock at the cave's mouth. She moved to him, touching his shoulder.

'I am well used to caring for children,' she said gently. 'I have worked with the nuns of the convent of St. Dominic in Salisbury—among the poor and at their own orphanage. Also, as you know, I speak good French.' He shook his head slowly from side to side, till, exasperated,

50

Abigail said sharply: 'I really do not see that you have a choice, sir! Now that I know your secret, am I not a potential threat to your safety?'

She heard him take in his breath sharply as he rose to his feet. 'You would betray me?' He looked down into her eyes.

She looked straight back at him, her own eyes flashing with their points of golden fire. 'Do you wish to test me, sir?'

He grasped her shoulders. 'I do not believe that you would risk harm coming to the children,' he said levelly, 'even if you care nothing for my safety.' He stared at her for a moment then began to laugh quietly. 'I can see that I would have a formidable accomplice in you, Mademoiselle—and an even more formidable enemy! Very well, let it be so. You are right—there is need for a woman in our work and you shall be that woman—but be warned—if you should put any of us in peril I will not hestiate to make you sorry you ever entered the venture. Is that clearly understood?'

She nodded firmly, hear heart beating fast with excitement. 'It is, sir. And now will you tell me what I have to do?'

He opened his mouth to spcak, but the sound of distant voices made him stop and listen. He stepped forward, lowering his voice and speaking rapidly:

'Can you meet me tomorrow morning—at

sunrise, on the hill above the village? Do you know the place they call the Dancing Maids?' She nodded breathlessly and he put a hand under her chin, lifting it to look into her eyes. 'If you are not there I will know that you have changed your mind. It would be understandable.'

Her eyes were bright and clear as they looked into his. 'I will be there, sir, never fear.'

For a moment they gazed at each other, their eyes locked, then the voices were heard again, closer now.

'Quick!' he said. 'The Dancing Maids at sunrise—till then.'

Abigail hurried across the sands and hastened up the cliff path, glancing once or twice over her shoulder at the dark figure standing at the cave mouth, a little spiral of excitement stirring in the pit of her stomach. Life at Broomcott promised not to be so dull after all!

CHAPTER FOUR

Bess crept stealthily up the back stairs and along the landing, pausing to count as she heard the church clock strike the hour—one—two—she was later tonight. Her stolen moments with Jack stretched longer each time she crept out to meet him. Tomorrow she would be falling asleep over her work again, cuffed and scolded by Sarah. Still, it was worth it. Her eyes grew dreamy as she recalled the warmth of Jack's kisses. 'If my luck holds we'll be able to be wed soon,' He'd said eagerly, showing her the purse of coins that was his night's wage. 'Just a little longer, love, and we can be together for always.'

She reached the door of her room and slipped inside, but as she turned a small cry escaped her lips. Someone was sitting on her bed—there, in the corner where the moonlight stopped short and the shadows began. She stepped back, her hand reaching for the door latch, her heart beating rapidly. The figure stood up and stepped into the moonlight.

'Bess—Bess, don't be afraid. It's only me.' Abigail put out her hand.

Bess let out her breath in a gasp of relief. 'Oh, Miss Abi! You'll be the death o' me! Why aren't you asleep in your own room?'

Abigail took the girl's arm and drew her away from the door and into the room. She still wore Arthur's clothes, but Bess noticed that she had washed her face and combed her hair. Her brown eyes were alight with excitement and Bess's heart sank. That look usually meant trouble for her!

'Listen, Bess,' Abigail pulled her down so that they were sitting side by side on the narrow bed. 'Can you help me to saddle my uncle's horse?'

Bess's mouth dropped open in amazement. 'Your uncle's horse, Miss Abi? What do you want wi' your uncle's horse?'

'I want to *ride* him of course!' Abigail retorted. 'I can ride, though I haven't had the opportunity since I've been here. I've a notion to ride up to the Dancing Maids to watch the sun come up.'

Bess drew in her breath sharply, gaping at her mistress. Had she taken leave of her senses? 'The Dancing Maids?' she echoed. 'You don't want to go up there, Miss Abi. Not when it be dark. They do say it be haunted up there. It's where Moll Tyson's cottage is.'

'Who is Moll Tyson?' Abigail asked.

Bess bit her lip. 'She were a wise woman— at least, she was once. Then her cures started working wrong way. 'Twas said she put curses on the village children. They began to die like flies. Then three that had died over to Mortstone was seen looking out o' her window—a week after they was laid to rest in the churchyard!' Bess's eyes were wide with horror. 'That was when they ducked her.'

It was Abigail's turn to gape. 'You mean— they drowned her? Without a trial—without giving her a chance to defend herself?'

Bess nodded vigorously. 'Afore she had time to put her evil eye on *all* of us!'

'Poor soul.' Abigail crossed herself. 'What she must have suffered.'

'What about them poor little 'uns, then?'

Bess asked indignantly. 'Anyway, since it happened they do say her spirit haunts the place—a' seekin' revenge, like.' Bess's eyes were round. 'No one won't go up there after dark.'

'I will!' Abigail stood up and threw her travelling cloak around her shoulders. 'Will you come and help me to saddle Uncle's horse? Then you must get some rest. I'd do it myself only he's so big, I don't think I could manage.' She grasped Bess's arm. 'Oh, do come on, girl! I want to get back here before it's light.'

Bess took a deep breath. 'Oh, very well, Miss. If you must go then I s'pose I'd better come wi' you.'

'No!' Abigail stared at her, aghast. 'I must go alone—I mean—I'd rather go alone. It'll be more of an adventure. And anyway, you need your rest.'

They made their way silently down to the kitchen and through the buttery. On the way Abigail took an apple from the store for Marcus, her uncle's big bay hunter. He was no stranger to her. She had been to visit him often in his stable, talking quietly to him and stroking the warm velvet nose. Apples, she knew, were his favourite treat and she looked forward now to the experience of riding him for the first time.

Bess grumbled all the time under her breath. 'I don't know what do get *into* you,

Miss Abi. Why do you always want to do such outlandish things? I always thought that young ladies of quality spent their time goin' visitin' and sewin' and the like. Why won't you let me come wi' you? An' what am I to tell the Master if you in't back by breakfast. He'll be mortal riled if he finds that Marcus gone!'

At last Abigail turned on her. 'Oh, do stop it, Bess! No harm will come to me, you can be sure. I'll be in my bed and Marcus in his stable by the time you're awake. Now, hold your tongue, *do*!'

Marcus gave a soft whinny when he saw Abigail and crunched his apple delightedly, making no protest when the two girls saddled him. He was a huge horse and Abigail needed Bess's assistance to mount him, but once she sat astride the broad back she felt safe and comfortable, excited too at the prospect of her meeting with the dark-eyed stranger she had met on the beach. Bess stood back, muttering disapprovingly.

'It's not lady-like, ridin' like that. I don't know—don't know, I'm sure.' She opened the stable door reluctantly. 'You be sure and be back like you said, Miss. I'll not know what to say if you'm not. And mind what you'm a'doin'.'

Abigail walked Marcus across the yard and out through the gateway into the lane, then she let him have his head, urging him towards the hill that rose behind the village like some dark crouching monster. Across the fields they went, the wind tearing the hood from Abigail's head and billowing her cloak out behind her. Her spirits soared and she wanted to laugh and shout into the wind.

When they reached the hill Abigail dismounted and quietly led the hunter to the shelter of a tall hedge, then, securing him, she made her way up the slope to where the tall stones were grouped in their crooked, shadowy circle. In the east the first pale streaks painted the dark sky but there was no sign of the stranger. She shivered as she looked around her. All was so still, then a small animal rustled the grass near her feet and the silence was broken by the distant unearthly cry of a vixen. On the brow of the hill she could see the outline of a small dwelling. That must be Moll Tyson's cottage. It looked black and sinister in the darkness and for the first time Abigail gave some thought to Bess's stories. *Could* the place be haunted by the malevolent spirit of the woman they had drowned as a witch? She thrust the thought from her. What nonsense! She did not believe in ghosts—nor witches either for that matter. No doubt some coincidence or trick of nature had thrown suspicion on the poor unfortunate creature.

A sudden sound behind her made her spin round. It came from behind one of the stones, but though she peered through the gloom she could see nothing. She looked at the stones, standing in their circle, a grim reminder of the powers of darkness. A shiver went down her spine. This certainly was a place of enchantment, whether the legend were true or not.

Abigail turned again as once more she heard the sound, a kind of rustling, then she gave a small involuntary cry as a tall figure appeared, as if from nowhere, putting a hand on her shoulder firmly.

'Oh!'

'Don't be afraid—' his voice was low and steady. 'I couldn't be sure at first if it was you.' His eyes smiled down at her. 'You came then.'

'I kept my word—I always do,' she said, her head held high.

'I hope you will always feel so brave and sure,' he said. 'And that it is not just your thirst for excitement and—forgive me—your curiosity that spurs you on.'

Abigail drew herself up as tall as she was able. 'I am not a child, sir,' she retorted. 'A foolish infant, ready to scream and faint at the first sign of danger. You forget, my own father died at the hands of those—those animals. If I am—' He stopped her words, putting his fingers against her lips and shaking his head.

'Mademoiselle—if we are to work together you must understand that talk of that kind is to be avoided at all costs. There are spies everywhere—in the most unthought-of places. Such foolishness could cost the lives of

58

those we seek to help.'

She felt her cheeks burn. 'Of course—I am sorry,' she whispered, lowering her eyes.

His expression softened as he looked down at her. 'You are very young,' he said quietly. 'Are you sure you wish to continue with this? Why not go home and dream your sweet dreams—forget all about me and all you have seen tonight?'

She looked up at him indignantly. 'I am eighteen, sir! I wish to help. I will not let you down. Once you have told me what you wish me to do I will not betray your trust, I promise you. I would die rather!'

He looked down at her flushed cheeks and took her two small, cold hands in his, stirred and touched by her vehemence. 'Come then— and I will try to make the position clear for you.'

When she saw that he was leading her towards Moll Tyson's cottage it was all she could do not to hold back. She watched as he bent and took a key from under a stone near the window. The door swung back, creaking on rusty hinges and an odour of damp mustiness drifted out to them. Going inside, the stranger lit a rush dip that had been left on the table and motioned to her to sit down on one of the two stools in the room. Looking across the table at her he began:

'Time is short so I will be brief. First, I must tell you that part of the work expected of you must be done here in this cottage. The woman whose home it was and who helped us greatly in the past is now dead. She was put to death for witchcraft but she was innocent.'

'I have heard the story,' Abigail told him, her heart beating fast. 'I imagined it to be so, poor soul.'

He looked searchingly at her. 'Then I take it that you are not of a superstitious turn of mind? I am glad, but I must warn you that it was through helping us that this woman put herself at risk.' He leaned forward. 'There is no time to tell you the full story now. Briefly, the work we are engaged upon is bringing the children of political prisoners out of France and passing them on to sympathizers in England who will care for them until such time as it is safe for them to return.'

Abigail felt a thrill run through her veins. Her assumption had been right. She clasped her hands together. 'Oh, how wonderful. Please tell me—in what way can I be of help?'

'Your task will be simply to care for and comfort the children on the night of their arrival,' he told her. 'Until dawn when they will continue on their journey.'

She looked around her in distaste. In the flickering light the room looked bare, comfortless and dirty, 'Here?' she asked. 'In this hovel?'

He nodded, smiling ruefully. 'That will also be part of your duty—to make it comfortable as best you can. There is a room above this where the children can be put to bed. When they arrive they are usually exhausted and hungry.'

Thinking of the plight of the children, Abigail immediately forgot her distaste for her surroundings. Then a thought struck her:

'But, sir—if poor Moll Tyson was taken for a witch is it safe to continue using this cottage?'

He nodded. 'There is nowhere safer! Since poor Moll's demise there are few people who will venture up here after dark. There are even rumours of hauntings.' He smiled grimly. 'I have made sure of them.'

Her eyes opened wide. 'You have?'

His dark eyes twinkled with merriment. 'It is easy, a word here and there in the right ears. Rumours grow faster than spring lambs in the country! You can be assured—this is the safest place for miles around.'

They laughed together and Abigail thought how handsome the stranger opposite was when the lines of his face relaxed into laughter. Though his dark eyes were serious, sometimes even grim, a smile was never very far from them. She liked the way he wore his own thickly waving hair and the promise of power in his broad shoulders. 'Shall I be seeing much of you, sir?' she asked shyly.

His eyes twinkled at her. 'Would it be so very hard for you to bear?'

61

She blushed warmly. 'Oh, no! I was merely thinking that it will be difficult for me to know how to address you. I do not know your name—nor you mine.'

'And it is better so, believe me,' he said gravely. 'Though I agree that we must call each other something. To my confederates on both sides of the channel I am known as "Roget". As for you,' he looked at her, his head on one side and the corners of his mouth twitching, 'As our leader is known as the "Eagle" it seems only fitting to me that you should be the "Wren". So I shall call you simply, "Jenny". Will that do?'

She smiled. 'It will do very nicely, I think.'

He rose and went to the window with a sudden urgency in his step. 'I must go. It is getting light.' He turned to her and held out his hand. 'Come, Jenny—home with you now. I will get a message to you when I need you. In the meantime I leave the cottage in your care. Do with it what you can.'

Outside the sky was streaked with pink and grey and the birds were already greeting the day. As Roget fastened his cloak he looked down at Abigail thoughtfully.

'One thing more before we part,' he said. 'The woman who told you there was to be a "cargo"—your maid?'

'Bess? You have no need to fear her,' she assured him. 'I shall tell her nothing of what has passed between us. She knows little or

62

nothing of your work. Her only concern is for her sweetheart, Jack. And she would do nothing to endanger him, you can be sure.'

He shook his head doubtfully. 'She may do so unwittingly. A little knowledge can be a dangerous thing.'

'Bess is not a fool,' Abigail said firmly. 'She is kind, loyal and intelligent. I would trust my life to her.'

He smiled down at her earnest face. Standing there in those ill-fitting, unbecoming clothes she looked oddly endearing. 'You are a good friend, Jenny,' he said. 'I only wish I had one half as good and true.'

She watched as he strode down the hill and mounted his horse. As he turned the animal's head towards the Dorchester road he looked back and raised his hand to her in farewell. She waved back. 'I shall be your good, true friend,' she whispered fervently. 'I will be true and loyal to you for as long as you need me.'

When he was out of sight she went back to the cottage and made sure they had left no trace of their visit, putting the key under the stone she had watched Roget take it from. Returning to Marcus she scrambled on to his back and made her way home. As they galloped across the fields her heart was beating fast. What if Jed or Sarah were already stirring? Would she get Marcus back into his stall and unsaddled without being seen? What had yesterday been little more than a prank, was now of life-and-death importance.

Luck was with her. As she reached the Manor stable yard the church clock struck the half-hour. Without too much difficulty she managed to unsaddle Marcus and left him solemnly watching her as she crept across the yard, grey in the dawn light and through the buttery. Up the back stairs she went, avoiding the creaking tread near the top—along the landing to her room and she was safe. Once in her room she gratefully shed Arthur's clothes and pulled on her nightgown. Then she slipped between the cool sheets and closed her eyes to ponder excitedly over all that had happened.

'Roget,' she whispered experimentally to herself. How *would* he get a message to her, she wondered when he didn't know her real name? When would it be and how would she get up to Maid's Hill next time? She might not be able to avail herself of her uncle's horse another time. Tomorrow she must try to think of a way. Tomorrow she would have a lot of thinking to do, but now she must try to sleep. Drowsily she wondered how old Roget was and whether he had a wife or a sweetheart somewhere. She hoped not—quite forgetting the fact that she herself was betrothed. To her surprise the thought of Roget's heart being engaged elsewhere was quite unthinkable to her.

'Roget' she whispered again and slept as the first pale gold rays of the morning sun crept over the window sill.

CHAPTER FIVE

'Miss Abi! Oh, Miss Abi, will 'ee wake up for pity's sake!' Bess shook her shoulder vigorously.

Slowly Abigail opened her eyes. 'What—what time is it?'

'It wants but a quarter to seven, Miss. And you know how cross your uncle do get if you'm not at table when he comes down.'

Abigail sat up and stretched, yawning sleepily. 'It only seems a moment ago that I went to sleep,' she complained.

Bess bustled about the room, picking up Arthur's clothes from the floor where Abigail had dropped them and gathering together the garments she must put on this morning.

'Make haste, do,' she urged. 'If you go gaddin' about all the night long you must expect to be sleepy—I know *I* am,' she added ruefully, stifling a yawn.

Abigail climbed out of bed. She was stiff, no doubt from her fall on the cliff path and from the unaccustomed riding.

'Ow!' She stretched her aching limbs each in turn, yawning again. 'I must get my uncle to let me ride again. I am out of practice it seems.'

Bess giggled. 'If you ask me, Miss Abi, you

65

does what you wants to do, whether your uncle do say so or not!' She looked at Abigail as she helped her on with her dress.

'And how did the Dancin' Maids look in the sunrise then, eh?'

'Very impressive,' Abigail said. 'I even took a look inside Moll Tyson's cottage.'

Bess gasped and stared at her mistress in horror. 'You mean you went right *in* there? You wants to be careful Miss. They do say that even a witch's spirit can put a curse on you!'

Abigail was about to scoff at Bess's superstitious beliefs when she remembered what Roget had said. A little fear was a healthy thing as far as Maid's Hill was concerned. She adjusted her expression to one of uncertainty.

'Can it really, Bess?' she asked, her eyes round. 'I must say that the place had an eerie feel to it.' That, at least was true, she told herself wryly.

When she reached the dining-room her uncle was already seated at the table, his fingers drumming impatiently on the arm of his high-backed chair. He glowered at her as she entered the room.

'Where the devil have you been, girl?' he barked. 'I've been waiting here these past ten minutes. D'ye think I've time to burn?'

A pert rejoinder rose to Abigail's lips but she bit it back. She had a favour to ask her uncle this morning so she would do well to stay on the right side of him.

66

'I am sorry I am late, Uncle,' she said demurely. 'I am afraid I did not sleep well and I was tired when it was time to rise.'

'Huh!' he grunted. 'Only one reason for not sleeping at your age—lack of exercise—not enough to do!'

Annoyance raged in Abigail's breast. Not enough to do indeed! When she had slaved long hours to make the Manor House a fit place in which to live! Then suddenly her anger cooled. She saw that her uncle was unwittingly giving her just the lead she needed for her request.

'Oh, I am sure you are right, Uncle,' she said, taking her place at the table. 'I have thought so for some time and I have been wondering if it would be convenient for me to have a horse of my own so that I could go for an afternoon ride—to familiarize myself with the countryside and take exercise.'

Thomas Hargreaves looked up at his great-niece in surprise. 'A horse? I had no idea that riding was a pursuit you enjoyed.' He considered for a moment, his lips pursed. As future mistress of Broomcott Manor and wife of his stepson Philip Jefferson, it was only right that the girl should become known about the place. Besides, if the villagers had a pretty young woman to look at and talk about, it would take their minds off their grievances and tiresome complainings. He nodded slowly, lifting his knife and fork to make a start on the breakfast that Bess was placing before him.

'Mmn—I don't see why not. Keep you out of mischief. I think there's a cob somewhere about that you might have. Speak to Harker about it. Tell him I said so. You seem to be on good terms with the fellow.'

Abigail gave him a brilliant smile. 'Oh, thank you, Uncle. I'll go as soon as breakfast is over.'

Bess, hovering about the table, caught Abigail's eye and gave her a knowing look which Thomas almost intercepted as he reached for a slice of bread.

'What are you doing, girl?' he thundered. 'Get about your business in the kitchen and stop gaping. Off with you now!'

As Bess scuttled from the room he looked across at Abigail. 'You must try to keep that girl in line more, niece.' He cleared his throat and laid down his knife and fork. 'You may be pleased to hear that we have received an invitation to dine at the Parsonage with the Reverend Wilford and his family. I had thought to refuse, but it occurred to me that you might enjoy such an occasion.'

As a matter of fact nothing of the sort had occurred to Thomas. When Parson Wilford had called on him the other evening to extend the invitation he had been deeply suspicious of the motive behind it. Wilford had a daughter who had recently completed her education at some fancy school. The girl had spent some time with a relative in London but had returned home with no prospects of marriage. It seemed obvious to Thomas that Wilford was now seeking a good match for the girl here in Broomcott and who was more eligible than Thomas's stepson, Philip? The two had known each other as children and had met once or twice in London, so Wilford had informed him. There was another reason too, if Thomas was not mistaken: Miles Wilford, the parson's odious son, had had his eye on Abigail for some weeks. He had noticed his furtive glances at her in church on Sundays. A handsome girl like Abigail would make an admirable wife for the slimy little toad and for the moment it suited Thomas to let the parson hope for success in his connivings. He had never liked or got along with him, but he could not deny that the man would make a valuable ally. The villagers seemed to consider him second only to the Almighty and would listen to him if he told them that Thomas's enclosure plans were the 'Will of God'. No doubt they would accept them quietly enough if the parson told them to.

He looked up to see how Abigail viewed the invitation and was irritated to find her day-dreaming, a far-away look in her golden-brown eyes.

'Did you hear what I said, girl?' he snapped. 'We are invited to dine at the Parsonage tomorrow evening. I thought it would be agreeable for you to meet other young people. Mr. Wilford has a son and daughter of your own age. Well—what do you say, child?'

Two thoughts were whirling in Abigail's head: would Parson Wilford recognize her as the 'lad' who had spilt ale all over him in the Dolphin that night? And suppose she received a message from Roget tomorrow? The latter she recognized must be a constant hazard and she must deal with it when it occurred; the former—she must just hope that the parson would not connect her with the Dolphin or its associations. She managed to smile sweetly at her uncle.

'I shall be delighted to dine with Mr Wilford and his family, Uncle,' she said. 'Indeed my only anxiety is for what I shall wear.'

Thomas grunted somewhat more amicably. 'Is *that* all?' He waved his hand vaguely. 'Wear that blue thing—the one with the lace fripperies. It will serve.' He leaned forward, his brow furrowed. 'One thing though: I think at this time it would be wiser to say nothing of your betrothal to Philip. After all you have not made his acquaintance yet and until you have, your betrothal cannot become official.' He cocked an eye at her. 'Do I take it that you agree?'

She nodded. Indeed, the engagement was something she would far rather forget and had no wish to discuss with anyone. 'It shall be as you wish, Uncle,' she said, her lashes lowered

70

in maidenly submission.

Broomcott Parsonage stood on the edge of the village behind the church. It was a small but handsome house, built within the last fifty years by a local church benefactor to replace the crumbling building that had served many previous generations of incumbents. Square and solid, with elegant long windows and a handsome porticoed doorway, it stood among elms and gracious lawns. As they drove up the wide carriage drive in the brougham kept for special occasions Thomas looked about him and snorted irritably:

'Huh! The fellow lives well—no doubt the tithes he collects pay for all this as well as filling his belly and putting good clothes on his back.' He glanced at Abigail's amused expression and added hurriedly: 'Not that I grudge the man any of it even though it does make the Manor look poor. No doubt the good man works hard among his flock.' He had no wish to implant to notion in Abigail's mind that there was any animosity between him and Parson Wilford.

As they drew up before the front door the Reverend Frederick Wilford came out to meet them.

'My dear Hargreaves,' he beamed, his ruddy face glowing 'How very gracious of you to dine with us.' He held out his hand to assist Abigail down from the brougham. 'And your charming niece, Miss Labeque. May I present my

71

daughter, Rebecca, and my son, Miles?'

Rebecca came forward first. She was a large, ungainly girl of about twenty with red hair and very white skin. Her eyebrows and lashes were so pale as to be almost indistinguishable and across her nose and forehead was a liberal peppering of freckles. Her dress she wore was an unfortunate shade of purple. She held out a plump, white hand to Abigail, her eyes flickering enviously over the crisp brown curls, dancing eyes and creamy complexion.

'I hope I find you well, Miss Labeque,' she said in a thin, nasal voice.

Abigail smiled. 'I am in excellent health, thank you. Won't you please call me Abigail?'

From behind his sister stepped Miles Wilford with some impatience. Was his sister going to stand there all evening, blocking his view with her bulk? He was as thin as his sister was plump, but with the same fiery hair and pallid skin. His pale blue eyes devoured Abigail greedily as he took her hand. At school he had encountered no woman at all except his headmaster's wife, a grey-haired lady of fifty. Indeed, his only first-hand experience of the fair sex came from his sister, Rebecca, with whom he quarrelled constantly. He had always believed, however, that somewhere he would find the woman of his dreams, the one he had read of in poems and novels and at his first sight of Abigail in church a few weeks ago, he

72

felt sure he had found her. Now his perspiring hand squeezed hers eagerly.

'I am most *charmed* to meet you, Miss Labeque—er—may I also have the honour of calling you by your delightful Christian name?'

Abigail nodded, withdrawing her hand gently from his over-long moist grasp. Miles Wilford gave her a feeling of distaste with his pale bulging eyes and fleshy lips. The way he hovered, stooping over her, made her feel that at any moment he might take a bite out of her neck. He reminded her of nothing more than a lizard in his green coat and the high cravat into which his chin disappeared.

'Please do,' she said faintly, looking at her uncle. Just at that moment she would have been glad to escape behind a confession of her betrothal and put a distance between her and the amorous Miles once and for all. But she had no doubt that her uncle had good reasons for wanting to keep it a secret.

The meal was excellent and Abigail made several mental notes of the dishes they enjoyed, to be tried out in the Manor kitchen in the near future. As they finished their dessert Rebecca rose and looked at her.

'Shall we leave the gentlemen to their port, Miss Abigail?'

Abigail followed her to an attractively furnished drawing-room where coffee was set out on a table before the fireplace. Rebecca indicated a chair.

'Will you take your coffee with cream and sugar, Miss Abigail?'

'Yes please—and do call me Abigail without the Miss,' Abigail urged. 'I hope that we shall be friends.'

Rebecca nodded politely, handing her a cup and seating herself opposite. 'I hope so too,' She cleared her throat. 'Do you find Broomcott to your liking, Mi—er—Abigail? It is an exceedingly dull place and the life here must be very different from the one you led at the convent where you were at school.'

'It is a different life,' Abigail agreed. 'I miss the people we cared for very much, especially the children.'

Rebecca put down her cup to stare at Abigail. 'You—*cared* for people and children? What kind of school could that have been?'

'The usual kind,' Abigail told her calmly. 'But when my papa could no longer despatch money across the channel to pay for my education I worked with the nuns instead— both outside with the poor and in their orphanage.'

Rebecca gave a delicate shudder. 'Oh dear, how very unpleasant for you—to be plunged into poverty and to be forced to do menial work. It was fortunate that your uncle was able to rescue you from such a life—fortunate indeed.'

It was all Abigail could do to bite back the retort that she would feel infinitely more useful working with the deserving poor than hob-nobbing with pasty-faced, self-appointed 'gentry' such as Rebecca! Instead, she smiled her sweetest and asked:

'Do tell me what you have done since you left school, Rebecca. I hear you have been staying with an aunt in London.'

Rebecca simpered, her small green eyes almost disappeared in folds of flesh. 'Oh, yes. She gave me a most elegant time—parties and balls and of course, the opera.' She put down her cup and looked directly at Abigail. 'It was at the opera that I was presented to your stepcousin, Philip Jefferson. Of course we knew each other as children but we had not met for some years.'

Abigail looked at her with interest. Her pale face had turned an amazing beetroot colour. Rebecca bit her lip and leaned forward confidentially.

'He has grown to be a very handsome man, as you no doubt know.'

Abigail shook her head. 'I have never set eyes on him.'

Rebecca's eyes glinted. 'Then—the rumours are not true?'

'As I do not know to what rumours you refer I cannot say, can I?' Abigail said sharply.

The colour deepened in Rebecca's cheeks. 'Of course, I never listen to servants' gossip— but our kitchen girl heard that you and Philip Jefferson were to be married.'

Abigail laughed lightly. 'But I have just told you: I have never set eyes on my cousin.'

'Of course.' Rebecca looked immensely relieved. 'I knew it was unlikely. After all, you have hardly been brought up to his kind of life, have you?'

Abigail moistened her lips. 'If what I have heard about his demeanour is correct I would indeed hope not!' she retorted. 'But then, like you, dear Rebecca, I never listen to servants' gossip!'

She smiled, her eyes flashing golden in the firelight and the smug expression vanished from Rebecca's face. She opened her mouth to say something but was silenced as the door opened and Miles came in, smiling his sickly smile.

'Father felt that you might like to be entertained. So I have come to—er—entertain you.' He stretched his chin clear of the cravat and sat down close to Abigail. 'Do you play or sing, Miss Abigail? I am sure we would be charmed if you would give us a sample of your talents.'

'I thought it was *you* who were to do the entertaining,' Rebecca snapped.

Miles turned a fish-like stare on her. 'I am sure you are tired of my poetry recitals, sister. As for me, I would welcome the sound of a sweet voice. Yours, I must confess, puts me in mind of a sick donkey!' He turned his attention to Abigail, his features resuming their leering smile as his damp hand reached for hers. 'Come, let me show you our new piano. I think you will find its tone quite pleasing.'

The piano's tone was pleasing to Abigail, at least, more pleasing than the voices of Miles and Rebecca. Also, while Miles's hands were engaged in its playing she was spared their clammy touch. She sang two songs and it was during the second of these that they were joined by the Reverend Wilford and Thomas Hargreaves. They seated themselves quietly in a far corner of the room where the parson smiled and nodded in time to the music.

'What a handsome couple they make,' he observed benignly. 'Your niece is a great credit to you, Mr. Hargreaves. A most handsome young woman. Not pure English, of course, but one would hardly know it to look at her.'

Thomas fumed inwardly. The fellow would begin to talk of dowries—next no doubt he intended to use Abigail's mixed blood as a bargaining point! For two pins he'd give the sanctimonious rogue a piece of his mind—but he must hold his tongue and play his cards close to his chest for a while. He forced his hard features into what he imagined to be a benevolent smile.

'She is indeed a blessing to me in my declining years,' he droned hypocritically. 'A pleasure to look upon and a delight to be with. The man who marries her will be blessed a hundredfold, though I could not allow it until she is older, of course.'

Mr. Wilford looked somewhat crestfallen. 'My dear wife was but seventeen when we were wed,' he said. 'Indeed when she was your niece's age she already held our son in her arms.'

Thomas sucked in his cheeks thoughtfully. 'Ah—but she had a mother to school her in wifely duties, no doubt. My poor Abigail has been with the nuns all these years and must be more familiar with the ways of the world before I can part with her. I would not have her marry unschooled.'

Thomas's 'poor Abigail' glanced across the room in his direction. She had finished the song and was afraid that Miles would at any moment suggest a walk in the garden or something. If only her uncle would announce that it was time to depart for home. But to her intense annoyance he avoided her eye and a moment later her fears were confirmed when Miles bent to speak, his lips almost touching her ear:

'Would you care to see the conservatory, Miss Abigail? We have a most interesting collection of tropical plants, some with the most exquisite flowers.' He gazed eagerly into her eyes. There seemed no escape.

She swallowed hard. 'I—I would be delighted—if Rebecca will join us.' She glanced towards the other girl, who stood up,

78

shooting her brother a malacious, triumphant look and crossed the room to join them.

Thomas Hargreaves hardly seemed to notice the departure of the young people. He had just managed to steer the conversation round to his farming plans and the ignorance of the village folk who did not recognize progress and God's goodness when they saw it.

The conservatory faced south and looked out on to the wide green lawns of the Parsonage. Miles had not exaggerated when he had described the plants. They were varied and exotic but after ten minutes of hearing their names, histories and origins, Abigail could scarcely conceal her boredom—as Rebecca was quick to notice.

'Can you not see that your tedious chatter is tiring our guest, brother?' she said acidly. 'Indeed, she can hardly keep from yawning. Can you not think of a more amusing topic of conversation?'

Miles's pale face reddened. 'I was about to compare Miss Abigail's beauty to that of the flowers,' he said stiffly.

Rebecca threw back her head and laughed shrilly. 'How typically lacking in observance you are! Have you not noticed that most of the blooms are of garish colours and bear a strong, pungent odour?'

Miles's colour deepened from red to purple as his embarrassment changed to anger. 'Then perhaps I should liken their charms to your own, sister!' he said with seething fury.

Rebecca's stout bosom seemed to swell alarmingly, her colour matching that of her brother. With a snort of rage she turned on her heel and swept out of the conservatory, which was exactly what Miles had hoped for. With his sister's departure his anger seemed to evaporate and he turned to Abigail apologetically.

'You must forgive our bickering,' he said smoothly. 'We have never agreed, even as children. But that need not concern you. Come, let me show you the garden, it is not yet quite dark.' He opened a door that led out on to the lawn, but Abigail held back.

'I really think I should be getting back to my uncle,' she said. 'He loses track of all time when he is enjoying himself, but he is not accustomed to late hours and needs his rest.'

Miles closed the door and stepped up close to her. 'Your concern for your uncle does you credit, Miss Abigail. Indeed I envy him. It must be a great delight to have someone as lovely as yourself to care for one.'

His pale eyes flickered over her speculatively as his hands reached out for hers. He pulled her gently towards him and his voice trembled as he said: 'For some time past I have admired your beauty, Miss Abigail. May I call on you soon? May I hope that you might welcome me?'

Abigail shook her head. 'I have a great

many duties to perform at the Manor. For the present it would not be convenient I think.'

He looked offended. 'Am I to take that as a rejection?'

'No—yes—no!' She felt her colour rise. 'The truth is that my uncle does not care for me to have callers—I have no female chaperon, you see.' This last was sheer inspiration and she heaved a sigh of relief. Miles's face relaxed.

'If that is all I could bring my sister.'

Abigail pulled her hands from his. 'I think I can hear my uncle calling. We had better return to the drawing-room.'

Reluctantly, he followed her but as soon as the door closed behind them Miles spoke to Thomas:

'I am most desolate, sir, to hear that you do not encourage your niece to have callers,' he said with a sidelong glance at Abigail. 'I am sure her life is very lonely. Will you not make an exception in my case?'

Thomas frowned at Abigail. 'Nonsense!' he barked. 'Welcome at any time, m'boy. Come when you like!'

And as Miles turned to Abigail, a triumphant smile on his fleshy lips, her heart sank.

CHAPTER SIX

'Then perhaps I should liken their charms to your *own*, sister!' Abigail mimicked Miles's voice and expression to perfection and Bess burst into fresh peals of laughter, holding her sides and protesting:

'Oh, Miss Abi, you'm a wicked 'un and no mistake, makin' game o' the parson's son like that!'

'Miles Wilford is no joking matter,' Abigail agreed. 'And if I am not very much mistaken we can expect him to call here any day now. Indeed, I am surprised that we have not had the pleasure of his company before.' Again she assumed Miles's slightly foppish stance, burying her chin in her neck: 'May I hope that you will welcome me, Miss Abigail?' she whined.

Bess giggled. 'So that's why you've been makin' yourself scarce these last few days then?'

It was partly true. Each afternoon since the evening at the Parsonage, Abigail had saddled Bobby, the sturdy little cob Jed had found for her and ridden up to Maid's Hill to do what she could to make Moll Tyson's cottage habitable. If Bess thought she went there to escape the attentions of Miles Wilford it was all to the good. It was now almost two weeks since her first meeting with Roget and as the days went by the episode grew more and more dream-like. Indeed, if it were not for the cottage and the work she had done there she might by now have come to believe she had dreamt the whole thing. How long, she wondered, would it be before there was another 'cargo'. And how *would* Roget get word to her?

She glanced at Bess. 'When do you expect to see Jack again?' she asked.

Bess shrugged. 'Sometimes there be weeks between cargoes, though Jack did say that they were hoping to bring more soon. I just looks for the rag tied to the old tree every day.'

Abigail thought about this. As things grew more desperate on the other side of the channel, parents were bound to become increasingly anxious for their children's safety. She wondered if Roget actually went to France for them, or whether he simply went out from this coast in the fishing boat to meet them midway.

'Bess—', she said thoughtfully. 'The man who organizes all this—does he go out with Jack and the others in the fishing boat?'

Bess shook her head. 'Jack don't tell me much, Miss, as you do know. But I think their gaffer—the one they calls Mr. Row-jay—do come across with the cargo—to see it safe like. Jack and the others, they picks up the cargo *and* him. Mind—', she wrinkled her brow.

'He'm not the *real* gaffer. Jack says he's someone important —a member o' the Parliament or some such. *That's* why he do be careful to keep secret like.'

'You'll let me know when there's a signal again, won't you, Bess?' Abigail said.

The girl bit her lip, looking uncertain. 'I *can't* take 'ee to the beach or the Dolphin again, Miss. Don't ask me to—*please*. Jack might lose this chance o' makin' extra money an' if that happens we'll *never* be wed!'

Abigail looked at the homely little face, creased with anxiety, the merriment quite gone from her eyes and she threw her arms round Bess in a sudden burst of affection.

'Dearest Bess! I would do nothing to make trouble for you and your precious Jack. I'd just like to know when you're seeing him, that's all!'

Bess looked into her mistress's eyes and saw that she meant what she said. 'You mean— you'd be content for me just to *tell* you about it, Miss Abi?' she asked incredulously.

Abigail nodded but Bess could not quite believe her. It wasn't like Miss Abi to take a back seat—*and* look so happy about it. No— she was up to something. Could it possibly be that she found Miles Wilford less repulsive than she made out? Maybe by avoiding him she was merely playing a game to make him keener. Bess certainly wouldn't put it past her!

They were engaged in clearing out the attic

and they had worked hard all the morning, carrying armsful of rubbish down to the yard for Danny, the skip-jack, to burn. Now, after lunch they were enjoying a short respite before beginning on the task of dusting and stacking the boxes and sweeping the floor. The attic ran the length of the house, with two small dormer windows looking out towards the sea and the two more on the other side, looking inland towards the village.

'This'd make a rare old look-out post,' Bess remarked, rubbing at one of the dusty panes with her apron. 'I do declare, you can see all the way to Mortstone. Oh—Miss Abi!' She bent forward, peering through the glass. 'I reckon that be Mr. Miles, comin' a'courtin'!' She giggled as Abigail pushed her out of the way.

'*Where*? Oh, Bess—say you're teasing me. He's not really coming, is he?'

But Bess was not teasing. There, coming across the fields by the bridle paths was Miles Wilford, riding a chestnut mare. True, he was but a minute figure from where they viewed him, but there was no mistaking the fiery hair and tall, stooping posture. Abigail flew across the room.

'Quick—he's a good two miles away yet. Come and help me saddle Bobby. I'll be gone in the other direction before he gets here.'

They ran down the back stairs and out to the stables, throwing the saddle on to an astonished Bobby's back in great haste.

'But what'm I to tell him when he gets here?' Bess asked, giggling.

'Oh—tell him I'm dead,' Abigail called climbing into the saddle, her skirts tucked up immodestly. 'Tell him—tell him I've flown away on a broomstick!' And digging her heels into Bobby's stout sides she was off across the yard and out of the gate, her hair flying behind her.

Bess bent to pick up her mistress's muslin mob-cap which had fallen unheeded into the mud. Well—that was one thought knocked on the head and no mistake. When Miss Abi had seen Mr. Wilford coming across the fields the look on her face had not been that of a maid in love—*that* it was not!

Once out of sight of the Manor, Abigail slowed Bobby's pace to a trot. She wanted time to think. Try as she may she could not understand her uncle's motives in allowing Miles to call on her when she was supposed to be betrothed to Philip Jefferson. It seemed totally against all his principles and even his explanation as they had returned from the Parsonage that evening had seemed inadequate.

He had need—he had told her—of Parson Wilford's support in his future plans. Unfortunately, the man seemed bent on encouraging a friendship between Abigail and his son and daughter but, he said, it was her duty to bear with him in the matter and to do nothing to discourage the attention of either of the Wilfords. He had been remarkably benign that evening—one might almost say wheedling—and she realized that her compliance must mean a great deal to him. She had toyed with the idea of telling Thomas of the rumours that Rebecca had heard concerning her betrothal to Philip, but she had quickly dismissed the idea. It could lead to Bess's dismissal and she could not bear that, knowing that the girl must be innocent. The author of the gossip was far more likely to have been Sarah. She supposed it was her duty to obey her uncle but the thought of Miles Wilford's pale, devouring eyes and clammy hands was too much. She would not offend him if she could help it but she would avoid him if she could.

She turned Bobby's head from the cliff path now to cross the fields on to the Dorchester road. As long as she was out she may as well go up to Maid's Hill and do a little more work at the cottage. She had found to her surprise on her first daylight visit that the tiny place had been well cared for. True it was dusty now from disuse but it was plain to see that Moll Tyson had once kept it as clean as a new pin. On previous visits Abigail had swept and dusted, scrubbing the flagged floor with water she brought from the stream at the foot of the hill. Upstairs in the small bedroom she had filled the mattress with fresh straw, brought from the Manor in small amounts each time she came, and only today she had put aside blankets and some old curtains she had found in the attic. When the latter were hung at the windows they would exclude any glimmer of light that might give away their presence.

Reaching Maid's Hill she tied up Bobby in the place she had found for him, a small clump of trees and bushes near the bottom of the hill. The view from up here was magnificent and she paused for a moment to enjoy it, savouring the cool, salty breeze on her face. Below, to the right, lay the village, looking for all the world like a cluster of toy houses. She could just glimpse the roof of the Parsonage rising from its rich green surroundings. Across the fields, the Manor stood, its tall chimneys dark against the blue of the sky. All around was the rich colour of field and common and ahead the sea lay, blue and sparkling in the sunlight, its small dancing wavelets capped with frothy white. Abigail breathed deeply, stretching out her arms—feeling free and exhilarated. Then she turned and ran up the hill, across the circle of stones, so harmless and ordinary looking in the light of day, and on up to the cottage.

Standing in the doorway, she surveyed the small domain with satisfaction. The flagged floor shone with cleanliness and in the wide hearth logs and kindling lay ready. She had scrubbed what cooking pots she could find as well as the mugs and wooden trenchers. The table and stools were dusted and the one small window polished till it shone. She climbed the rough stairway and looked at the slatted cot with its mattress of new straw. Yes, when she had brought the blankets and curtains all would be ready for the first refugees. She smiled in anticipation of Roget's pleasure and a vision of his handsome face filled her mind: the fine, dark eyes and broad forehead, the high-bridged, straight nose and finely moulded lips with their promise of humour. Everything about him spoke of strength. She sighed. How unlike Miles Wilford he was. If only it were Roget who wished to call and pay court to her. But it seemed their partnership was to be a purely platonic one. 'We are to work shoulder to shoulder in a noble cause', she told herself sternly—'One that has nothing to do with the foolish romantic fancies of a silly girl!'

With one last look round she closed the door, replacing the key in its hiding place under the stone, and started down the hill to the waiting Bobby. Not for the first time she wished she were able to take Bess into her confidence and enlist her help, but she knew that Jack had been right when he had said that the less Bess knew, the better. She would do nothing that would put her friend and maidservant in danger, even though she knew the girl would help her readily and without question if she were asked.

Bobby was pleased to see her, whinnying softly and nuzzling her shoulder as she untied the reins. She patted his woolly neck.

'One night soon we'll have a real adventure, boy, you and I,' she told him.

As she mounted, Abigail was aware for the first time of her mode of dress. Not having had time to change into her riding habit she wore the dress she had been working in all day, of plain grey cotton, its skirts tucked up. And her hair, free of its cap, blew loose in the wind, a mass of dark, tumbling curls. She hoped that no one would see her looking so wild and urged Bobby homewards across the fields. On the cliff path she stopped for a moment and looked out to sea.

'I'm ready for you, now,' she said aloud. 'I'm waiting. Come soon—oh *do* come soon!'

'It seems that some at least have the honour of a welcome from you, Miss Abigail.'

The voice startled her and she spun round to come face to face with Miles Wilford. He must have seen her coming across the fields and waited for her out of sight. She had certainly not heard him ride up.

'Oh—good afternoon, Mr. Wilford,' she said with as much dignity as she could manage.

He swept off his tricorne hat, his eyes sweeping over her as he took in her appearance: the tumbling curls, tangled by the wind, the pink cheeks and sparkling eyes, then down to the exciting expanse of shapely calf exposed by the tucked-up skirts.

'You must have left the Manor in a great hurry, Miss Abigail,' he said lazily, his fleshy lips curving. 'Could you have been avoiding someone, I wonder? Or perhaps expecting to meet someone?'

Discomforted by his eyes on her, Abigail turned her back and slid down from Bobby's back, shaking out her skirts and smoothing her hair as best she could. He laughed and leapt down from his own mount.

'Please, Miss Abigail, do not distress yourself on my account. I meant no criticism of your appearance I assure you. Indeed, you look quite charming—like a wood nymph or a gypsy girl.'

She felt herself flush. 'I am not sure, sir, whether that is complimentary or not!'

He smiled. 'But it was meant as such, I promise you.'

He was enjoying himself. Today he had the upper hand and he was quick to see it. The other evening in the conservatory at the Parsonage, Abigail had made him feel callow and inexperienced. Today was his chance to show her that he could be masterful. Unhurriedly he secured his mount and came over to where she stood.

'You have not yet explained how it is that you are here like this,' he said. 'Could it be as I said—that you are trying to avoid someone? I hope indeed that it could not have been me.'

His face assumed an expression of mock despondency. 'On the other hand—if the words I heard you speaking were—'

'I was merely thinking aloud,' she broke in. 'I am a creature of impulse. It was a beautiful day, the sun shone.'

'So you leapt on to your horse and rode away,' he finished for her, smiling cynically. 'What a delightful picture that conjurs up in the mind. Perhaps you will allow me to escort you home?'

She bit her lip. How could she refuse? 'Thank you, sir,' she muttered. 'Perhaps it would be better if we were to walk. My own saddle has not yet arrived and I fear this one is hardly suitable.'

He smiled down at her, his pale eyes gleaming at the memory of the shapely leg he had glimpsed. 'Nevertheless, you seemed to be managing remarkably well with it,' he said. 'Coming across the fields you might have been Diana herself. You looked quite abandoned and reckless.' He stepped up close to her and put his hands on her shoulders. 'One might almost have thought you had been to meet a lover.'

She flushed and shrugged his hands from her shoulders.

'Sir! It is quite improper for you to speak to me in this manner.'

But his grasp on her only tightened as he bent forward, his face close to hers. 'There is no one to see, Abigail—nor to hear. I have admired—no, *adored* you for so long. Tell me truly, has someone already claimed your affections? My sister says—'

'Your sister should not listen to gossip,' Abigail interrupted. She was utterly confused. If she admitted to her unwilling alliance with Philip Jefferson she would go against her uncle's wishes—if she denied it, she must put up with the attentions of Miles. 'My affections have been claimed by no one,' she said stiffly. 'And I have no wish that they should be. My uncle has sore need of me.'

He pulled her towards him and bent so close that she could feel his breath on her cheek. 'I have sore need of you, Abigail,' he said, his voice trembling. 'You cannot know the nights I have lain dreaming of you— longing for you. If only you would give me hope that you would someday return my love—'

Horrified, she pushed him away. 'Mr. Wilford! You are taking advantage of me in the most shameful way! Please let me pass. I shall go home alone!' Trembling, she mounted the cob, pulling her skirts down her legs as far as she could, then, digging her heels smartly into Bobby's flanks she moved away.

Miles watched her go, cold fury mounting in his breast. Who did she think she was? A half French orphan girl the Squire had taken pity on. A poor relation. What right had she to be so high and mighty? Riding about the countryside like a gypsy! Of one thing he was sure—he would find out what it was she was up to and make her pay for this afternoon's work. He replaced his hat and remounted his horse, moving off thoughtfully in the opposite direction. Perhaps his sister could think of a plan. There was no love lost between them, but she had her uses, one of them being her devilishly inventive mind. Oh yes, Miss Abigail Labeque would pay her debt. Pay it in full!

Abigail's heart beat fast as she rode away. No doubt she had offended him, but she could not help it. After all, he had taken advantage of her and she would tell her uncle so if he complained. One fortunate thing had come out of it at least: Miles must now know that she did not welcome his attentions and with luck he would trouble her no further—or at least, so she hoped.

Half an hour later she was grooming Bobby in his stall when Jed Harker came in and stood regarding her thoughtfully.

'You're pleased wi the little fellow then, are you, Miss Abi?'

She looked up and smiled at him. 'Oh yes, Jed. He's a darling and can go quite fast when I want him to.'

He moved close to the cob's side, his eyes meeting hers across the broad back. 'Let him rest awhile now, Miss,' he said quietly. 'He'll be needed again tonight.'

Her heart almost stopped as she stared at him. He nodded, answering her unspoken question.

'Be at the cottage by midnight,' he whispered.

Abigail was stunned. So that was it—*Jed* was the messenger—Jed, of all people! As he made to move away she reached for his hand.

'How did you know?' she asked in a whisper. 'Who told you it was me? I told him nothing—he wouldn't let me.'

Jed smiled and shook his head. 'You were described to me and I was told that you were new to the village. It could have been no one else, Miss.'

'Does *he* know who I am?' she asked.

'No,' he told her. 'Only I know—and I shall tell no one.' He glanced over his shoulder. 'Midnight then—take care, Miss Abi. God go with you.' And without another word he was gone.

The church clock was striking half past eleven as Abigail led Bobby quietly out through the yard into the lane. She was glad of his broad, sturdy back for she had much to carry. Rolled up and tied to the saddle were the blankets and curtains she had put by and in her hand she carried a basket containing bread, milk and a large stonewear jar full of hot broth she had made herself.

There was no moon and as she walked Bobby along the lane between the hedges all

95

seemed inky blackness. When they emerged on to the field path, however, she found that her eyes had accustomed themselves to the darkness enough for her to find the way. Tonight she wore a thick woollen dress and her heavy travelling cloak, the hood up to hide her face. She did not expect to encounter anyone, but it was better to be on the safe side.

Once out of sight and hearing of the Manor she mounted the little horse carefully and urged him forward, though even at a gentle trot it was all she could do to hold on to the reins and steady the basket too. At the foot of Maid's Hill she stopped, securing Bobby in his accustomed place. Then, carrying her burden, she made her way up to the deserted cottage, her heart quickening at the thought of the task before her.

She lit the candles she had brought with her and hung the heavy curtains at the windows, excluding any tell-tale glimmer of light, then she made up the bed with the blankets. She unpacked the food and set it out on the table along with the trenchers and mugs. When she had finished it all looked quite homely and she began to let her thoughts drift to what must be happening on the beach. In her mind she saw the boat coming in—the men pulling it into the cave, then going off to make sure the coast was clear. Roget would have a horse waiting somewhere—perhaps Jed would see to that. Then he would bring the children here to her.

Oh, she hoped all would go well!

Suddenly she started as she heard a noise not far away. Was it some animal stirring? No, it sounded like a step. Then there were muffled voices. Extinguishing all the candles but one she crept to the door listened—there came a tap and a voice asking softly: 'Jenny—are you there?' She threw the door open and there he was pushing two small children into her arms and closing the door behind them hurriedly.

When she thought about it afterwards that night seemed to Abigail to pass like a dream. Although they were almost too exhausted to eat, she fed the children and then put them to bed in the room upstairs. As she came down Roget looked up at her from the table where he sat tasting his own bowl of broth.

'This is very good. You have done well, Jenny.'

Her cheeks flushed with pleasure. 'I have done the best I could,' she said. 'I intended to light a fire and cook a meal but then I thought that the smoke coming from the chimney might give us away. I am glad the broth stayed hot in the jar.'

He nodded. 'It is excellent and I am sure it will have revived the children. It was clever of you to think of the smoke, but I think perhaps we might risk it on moonless nights.' He pushed the jar towards her. 'Will you have some broth yourself?'

97

She shook her head. 'You finish it. I dined earlier. You must be hungry and tired too. At what time must you leave?'

'No later than sunrise.' He sighed wearily. 'It is two nights since I slept. Each time I return to France the dangers seem more acute—and then on this side I am in constant fear of coinciding with the local smugglers.'

Abigail's heart contracted with concern for him. 'You risk your life for these little ones. You are very brave. Will you not try to sleep a little now?' She took a spare blanket to the high-backed settle by the fireplace. 'I am afraid there is no pillow but if you will you may rest your head in my lap.' She bit her lip, shyness suddenly overcoming her.

Roget stood up, towering above as his head almost touched the low ceiling. He placed his hands on her shoulders and his eyes glowed softly as he looked down at her. 'It sounds extremely inviting, Jenny, but I must stay alert, at least until I have safely delivered my charges and their legacies.'

She raised her eyebrows enquiringly. 'Legacies?'

'Yes.' He lifted the heavy saddlebag he had brought in with him and opened it. Inside she saw the glint of jewels and the dull glimmer of gold. 'My living charges are precious indeed,' he continued. 'But they are not my only responsibility as you see. This is their investment against a better future.' He put the saddlebag down and patted her shoulder. 'At least now we can break our journey and rest before continuing, thanks to you.'

For a while they talked. Abigail longed to ask Roget more about himself—about the children and the organization of which she was now a part, but she knew she must not. Instead, she asked him about poor Moll Tyson and how she came to meet her untimely end. Roget shook his head.

'It was tragic and unfortunate and I am afraid that the blame must rest entirely on me. Moll was a kind woman who knew how to make medicines and cures from herbs and plants. For years the local people had respected her and came to her with their ailments—and those of their animals too. Usually she was successful, but of course, not always. Around that time there was a sickness among the children. Moll did her best but a great many of them died and in their grief and desperation, the village folk turned on Moll. The terrible word 'witch' began to be bandied abroad. One night I brought three children across from France. As usual Moll fed them and when they had rested I rode with them to Dorchester as usual. My contact failed to meet me. I waited all next day but he did not appear. I was due back in London so I had to make a decision. I waited till dark and then brought them back here to Moll. When I got to London I made arrangements for them to be collected, but by then it was too late.'

'What had happened?' Abigail asked, round-eyed.

'A passer-by had caught a glimpse of the children looking out of the window,' he told her. 'The word went round like wild-fire that Moll was harbouring children she had taken from graves in the churchyard and brought to life again with the help of the devil. When an angry mob came up here and searched the place the children were gone, but that only made them more certain than ever that Moll was a witch. It was said that she had spirited them away.' He sighed. 'She was questioned and bullied—finally dragged away and drowned. Never once did she mention me or tell them the truth. She could have saved herself but she died rather than betray me.' He took Abigail's hand and looked into her eyes. 'So now you know what dangers you face, Jenny, and the cruel reason why we must know as little as possible about each other.'

She nodded. 'I understand.'

'And it does not dismay you?' He pressed the small, cold hand between his own two.

She lifted her face to him. 'Not while I can serve you—and the children of France. They are the future.'

He bent and gently kissed her forehead. 'Jenny—' he began, but a thin wail from upstairs sent her hurrying to the dreaming child.

As the first light began to appear in the east she roused the children, dressing them and feeding them with the milk and bread that was left in the basket. She did her best to hearten and encourage them, speaking to them in their native language, but it tore her heart in two when they cried pitifully for their 'maman'. She wished she could go with them on the rest of their journey, as she told Roget.

'Where will they go next?' she asked him, but he shook his head.

'I will ride with them to Dorchester and there hand them over to a man called Paul. I know no more than that. Each of us plays his own part in the operation without question. Our organization is based on trust, so that if one of us were caught we could give nothing away—even if we were tortured. Moll's death taught us that grim lesson.' Abigail shuddered. 'Please—please take care, Roget,' she whispered urgently.

'Oh, I will, you can be sure of that,' he told her ruefully. 'I am much too fond of this life to want to quit it yet.' He smiled down at her. 'But it is good to know that one so sweet and gentle—brave too—desires my safety.'

She walked with them to where Roget's horse was waiting and lifted the children up to him in the saddle. He enfolded them protectively with his cloak, then bent to touch her cheek.

'God bless you, Jenny. Till we meet again,

au revoir.'

She watched him guide his mount carefully down the hill and on to the road. She saw his profile etched against the pale sky, strong and handsome as he turned his head towards her for the last time. As she lifted her hand in farewell tears pricked her eyelids.

'Please take care,' she whispered. 'Take care—my dearest love.'

CHAPTER SEVEN

As she came out of the cottage overlooking the village green Abigail held up her hand to shield her eyes from the bright sunlight. It was a hot day and it had been stuffy inside the one low-ceilinged room of the cottage. She breathed the fresh air again gratefully. She turned to Mary Bray, Jed Harker's niece, whose child she had been asked to visit.

'I am sure it is nothing to worry about, Mary,' she said soothingly. 'I saw many children with similar rashes at St. Dominic's. It is not plague or disease. I will send you some milk from the goats at the Manor. Give it to little Matty to drink three times a day. I will make you a salve to apply to the sores too. It is made with goat's cream and lichen and you will soon see an improvement.'

The young woman looked doubtful. 'Goat's

milk, Miss Abigail? Surely if I give my babe that she will grow horns.'

Abigail laughed gently. 'Believe me, she will not. She can only thrive and grow well again, I promise. This cure has worked many times before. I have seen it with my own eyes.'

With a last farewell she turned towards home, her basket on her arm. It was now six weeks since her first secret night visit to Maid's Hill and there had since been two more 'cargoes' to keep her busy. Visiting the village people had filled the time in between. In their poverty there was great need for her healing skills though it seemed to her that the little she could do was pathetically inadequate. Since her uncle had laid off so many of his workers there was pitiful suffering. Many families were close to starvation and there were children with far worse illnesses than little Matty Bray.

Preoccupied as she was with her thoughts Abigail did not at first see Rebecca Wilford coming towards her along the road. She rode on a white pony and wore a riding habit of green velvet in which she looked extremely hot. Her eyes flashed with sparks of spiteful envy as they swept over Abigail in her cool spotted muslin and she could not quite keep the sharp edge from her voice as she called out:

'Abigail, my dear! It is quite providential that I should see you. I was on my way to the Manor to accept your kind invitation to dine.'

Abigail looked up in surprise. 'Oh, good day to you, Rebecca.' The mention of the coming dinner party brought her back sharply to her own problems. The occasion was one to which she looked forward without enthusiasm, though she had to admit that not to have returned the Wilford's hospitality would have seemed churlish. Her uncle seemed totally oblivious, however, of the inadequacies of the Manor kitchen. It would be on Abigail's own shoulders that the weight of responsibility would rest. She composed her features into a polite smile.

'I am so glad that you will be able to come,' she said. 'Though of course, we do not have the comforts that you are accustomed to at the Parsonage. I fear my uncle's bachelor existence has led him into rather frugal ways.'

Rebecca gave a short patronizing laugh. 'Pray do not apologize, Abigail, dear. We are well aware that the standard of living we enjoy is out of the ordinary. We do not expect to meet it in other country homes. Indeed we are glad to be able to bring a little luxury to the lives of others occasionally.'

Although the slight was not wasted on Abigail she smiled back sweetly, making up her mind at the same time that the Wilfords should eat the best dinner they had ever tasted at the Manor next week—though quite how she would get Sarah to produce it she did not yet know! She looked into Rebecca's small,

104

spiteful eyes.

'I am sure we shall do our humble best to please you,' she said demurely, inclining her head respectfully.

Rebecca looked at the basket on Abigail's arm. 'I take it you have been sick visiting again. You really should take care, Abigail. These people contract the most disgusting disorders.'

Abigail's eyes flashed. 'You are right, poor souls, and the fault lies mainly with their poverty which they cannot help. But if my small knowledge can ease their suffering a little I am glad.'

Rebecca sniffed delicately. 'How very noble of you.' She pointed to the toddler playing near the cottage door. 'Have you been treating *that*?' She wrinkled her snub nose.

'It is merely an infant skin complaint,' Abigail told her. 'There are far worse sufferings in the village than that. This can easily be cured by the drinking of goat's milk and the application of a salve made—' But Rebecca did not let her finish.

'The milk of a *goat*?' she repeated. 'How mightily interesting. Have you any idea how superstitious the people of this county are, Abigail?'

Abigail nodded. 'I am aware of that, but they trust me, I hope.'

A slow smile spread over Rebecca's plump features and her eyes glinted maliciously. 'We shall look forward to seeing you next Wednesday at eight then. Good-day.' And she turned her pony's head abruptly, leaving Abigail staring after her.

But if Rebecca's manner puzzled her the days that followed left her little time for speculation. Gathering together all the recipes she could remember she began to assemble the ingredients for the planned dinner party. She instructed Jed to obtain pigeons and rabbits for her and to gather fresh herbs and vegetables from the garden and on the day of the dinner she rode herself down to Mortstone to buy fresh fish from the fishermen as they brought their haul ashore. She was busy from dawn to dusk, scolding Bess and cajoling Sarah—preparing puddings and sauces and pastries until nothing occupied her waking hours but the meal, which she was so determined to make a success.

This state of affairs came to an abrupt end however on the Wednesday evening. Abigail was in the kitchen giving Bess and Sarah their final instructions before she went upstairs to change her gown when Jed came in and asked to speak to her. She followed him out to the stable yard where he beckoned her to a shadowy corner.

'Miss Abi—'tis short notice, I know, but you are to be on the beach at midnight tonight.'

Abigail gasped. 'Tonight? And on the *beach*—are you sure of this?'

He nodded. 'There be a young 'un expected—still in arms. Your help be sorely needed I reckon.'

She bit her lip. If only it were any night but this. Would the Wilfords be gone in time for her uncle to be in bed and asleep by midnight? She fervently hoped so.

'Very well, Jed,' she said briskly. 'Thank you for telling me.'

The meal went well and the Wilfords seemed to enjoy it. Even Rebecca admitted, though somewhat grudgingly, that Abigail's pigeon pie was a delight and her fruit syllabub melted in the mouth. Thomas Hargreaves nodded meaningly at Miles.

'My niece will make some lucky man a very accomplished wife, eh?'

Miles leered across the table at Abigail, his eyes lingering on the soft curve of her bosom at the neckline of her gown. 'Not only accomplished but desirable too,' he said thickly with a tone that made Abigail's flesh creep.

After dinner the two girls retired to the little-used drawing-room which had been specially dusted and a fire lit for the occasion. But in spite of these preparations a damp, musty smell pervaded the room and Rebecca wrinkled her nose, making her opinion all too clear. Bess brought in the coffee but Abigail had scarcely had time to pour before they were joined by Miles.

'It seems our elders are bent on talking of farming matters,' he said, smothering a yawn. 'And as sheep and cows bore me to distraction I thought I would see if your conversation was more entertaining,' he said languidly. He sidled up to Abigail and seated himself uncomfortably close to her. 'Perhaps I might beg a cup of coffee. I'm sure it will be as delicious as the rest of the meal—and as you are yourself, Abigail.' His hot, damp hand rested for a moment on her bare arm and Abigail moved away, only barely suppressing a shudder.

'Certainly you may have a cup,' she said coolly. But as she poured she noticed the look which passed between brother and sister. It puzzled her. She knew their relationship was not close and yet the look they exchanged was one of two people in conspiracy. As she passed the cup to Miles, Rebecca asked:

'How is the child whose rash you treated, Abigail?'

'Much improved, I am glad to say.' Abigail smiled.

Rebecca turned to her brother. 'The milk of a goat brought about this small miracle,' she said. 'Taken three times each day—and a salve applied, made from the goat's cream mixed with lichen. Wonderful, is it not? For all the world like a magic spell!'

Miles raised his eyebrows, the corners of his mouth curving sadistically. 'Not a *black* magic spell, I trust!'

'I confess it must sound remarkably like it to those of a superstitious nature,' Rebecca replied. 'The milk of a *horned beast* added to the mystic number—three!' She shook her head.

Abigail stared at her. 'You are surely not telling me that you believe in such nonsense? This cure was devised by the holy sisters of St. Dominic's.'

Rebecca's sandy eyebrows almost disappeared into her hair as she gave a dry mirthless laugh. 'My dear, that signifies nothing. In these parts witchcraft and popery go hand in hand!'

Miles's hand closed once more round her arm and he moved closer to her so that she could feel his breath upon her cheek as he spoke to her.

'I am greatly concerned for you, my dear Abigail. You really should employ great caution in dealing with these people. It is not so long ago that a woman in this very village was judged a witch and put to death for similar practices. I would hate to see such a fate befall one so lovely.'

Abigail caught her breath and moved away from Miles, standing up and crossing to take Rebecca's empty cup. 'I cannot take your warning seriously,' she said lightly, but as she caught the look that passed again between the Wilfords she felt a chill creep through her veins. A threat hung in the air between them like a black cobweb and she felt the skin on the back of her neck tingle.

'I cannot believe that I have enemies in the village,' she said sitting down again some distance from Miles.

Rebecca's eyes glinted. 'One can never be sure with these uneducated louts,' she said. 'They are so unpredictable. They will as soon turn and bite the hand that has fed them as breathe the air. It was always so, was it not?'

'I cannot say that I have ever experienced anything but gratitude,' Abigail said stoutly. 'The poor—I take it it is they to whom you refer—have always been appreciative of my small knowledge and experience.'

Miles's lips curled sardonically. 'Then let us hope that your cures continue to *cure* and that your good luck holds for it needs but one failure to dash their faith in your magic.'

Abigail's cheeks reddened. 'But I make no such claims,' she protested. 'I profess to be no more than a friend to them and help them as such only.'

'And you will be nothing less than their sworn enemy should one of them happen to die,' Miles said with a lazy smile.

'Come, brother. I do believe we are frightening poor Abigail,' Rebecca said, her small eyes glittering like green glass pebbles. 'Do let us talk of something else.' She eyed Abigail's neck. 'I see you are not wearing your pretty locket tonight, Abigail. I hope you have not broken it. If you have I can recommend an excellent jeweller.'

Abigail fingered the bare skin of her throat, reminded of something that had troubled her for some weeks. The locket Rebecca referred to had been a present from her papa when she first came to school in England many years ago. It carried a tiny miniature portrait of him and was engraved with her name. It had never left her neck since the day her father had given it to her but she had missed it after returning from Maid's Hill that first night. Although she had covered every inch of the ground the next day the locket was not to be found.

'It is not broken—at least, I suppose it must have been for I have lost it,' she said. 'I imagine it must have fallen from my neck somewhere outside.'

'What a pity,' Rebecca said disinterestedly, barely concealing a yawn.

Miles had been wandering restlessly round the room as they spoke and had now stopped near the old-fashioned spinet which stood in the corner. 'Will you not give us the delight of hearing you play again, Abigail?' he asked. 'I declare I have longed to hear you again since you played and sang to us at the Parsonage.'

Abigail rose reluctantly. She was not anxious to play her uncle's spinet, guessing that it would make sad comparison to the Wilford's fine new pianoforte, but she was even more reluctant to resume the unpleasant turn the conversation seemed to be taking. Seating herself at the instrument she flexed her fingers, eyeing the yellowed keys apprehensively.

Her fears were justified. The spinet jarred and jangled most horribly, much to the Wilfords' ill-concealed delight, and she was greatly relieved when the door opened and her uncle came into the room followed by Mr. Wilford who announced somewhat peremptorily that the time for departure had come. One look at her uncle's face was enough to tell Abigail that all was not well between him and the parson. Though he was making the greatest effort to be polite his wrinkled face was dark with displeasure.

All five moved to the front steps to await the Wilford carriage but while the others were occupied Miles took Abigail's arm and drew her a little to one side.

'I believe I heard you tell my sister that you had recently lost a trinket,' he said.

Involuntarily her hand flew to her throat. 'Yes,' she said. 'My locket. It is of great sentimental value to me. Do you know where it is?'

'I can do better than that.' Taking her hand he placed the locket in it, closing the fingers over it. Then he bent his head close to hers. 'But if I were to tell where and when I found it there might be some awkward questions asked.' He smiled conspiratorially. 'It shall be our secret, Abigail,' he whispered. 'Though of course I shall expect you to be more agreeable to me than you have of late.'

She felt her cheeks flush crimson. Where could he have found the locket and what did he think he knew? She lifted her chin.

'I'm afraid you speak in riddles,' she said defiantly. 'Though I am deeply grateful to you for the safe return of my locket. I ride out on most days and could have dropped it in any one of a hundred places.'

He smiled and raised her hand to his lips. 'I think we understand each other well enough, Abigail. But we will say no more for the present. We will meet again soon I can assure you.' And with a significant look he left her to join his father and sister in the carriage.

When they were out of sight Thomas Hargreaves let out a snort: 'Pah! Who does the fellow think he is?' He hurried back into the house as fast as his gouty leg would carry him, Abigail following closely behind him.

'Have you disagreed, Uncle?' she asked. 'I thought you and Mr. Wilford were such good friends.'

'Huh! Arrogant fellow!' This evening Thomas had broached the subject of the sermon he wished the parson to preach on his behalf, praising the progress and advances in farming methods. But his suggestions had met with little co-operation from the reverend gentleman. He had spoken of the riots and midnight firings that had occurred in other villages. Was the fellow a coward? Thomas fumed. Did parsons no longer do as their squires bade them? No doubt the fellow thought that because he had a private income—for that was the conclusion Thomas had come to—he could have the last word!

'Huh!' he repeated. 'We shall see what the Bishop has to say on the matter. 'Tis my opinion that Wilford is feathering his nest in some way from the villagers! Well, we'll see— we'll see!' He glared at Abigail. 'This evening's meal must have cost a small fortune. Why did you have to be so extravagant, girl? What do you mean by it, eh? Spending my money like water!'

Her eyes widened. 'It did not cost so much, Uncle. Most of the produce came from our own land. Besides, I thought it would be your wish to give the Wilfords a meal at least as fine as the one they gave us!'

His face paled from purple to brick red and he shook his head. 'Never again,' he growled between clenched teeth. 'Those people are not to set foot in this house again. See to it that they don't!' He lowered himself into a chair with a groan and Abigail went to him.

'But Uncle, you told Miles Wilford that he could call on me. Am I to take it that now—'

'You are betrothed to my stepson, Philip!' he thundered glaring at her with bloodshot

114

eyes.

Stunned, Abigail took a step backwards, shaking her head in bewilderment. 'But—you told me to make no mention of the fact. Indeed, you yourself encouraged Miles Wilford to call on me here—even this evening you—'

'Hold your tongue, girl!' He waved a hand impatiently at her. 'Do not be so perverse. An argumentative woman is like a thorn in a man's flesh. God forbid that I should shelter such a creature! Get off to your bed, Miss. From this night your friendship with the Wilford brats must cease—and I can't say I admire your taste in friends!'

Speechless, she stood rooted to the spot for a second, then she turned and ran up the stairs, her throat constricted with tears at her uncle's unfairness.

On the landing Bess had been waiting in the shadows for her mistress. She was going tonight to meet Jack and she had decided to ask Abigail if she would like to go too. It was some time since they had been out together and she had been puzzled that her mistress had not plagued her to go again. She had heard the master shouting and felt sorry. Miss Abi did not have much pleasure in this household. Perhaps she could bring a little excitement to her life for once. As Abigail passed she put out her hand.

'Miss Abi—can I speak to you? I've

somethin' to tell 'ee.'

But Abigail shrugged her off angrily, sweeping past the crestfallen girl and into her room, slamming the door behind her.

Inside she sat down on the bed to think. If only her uncle had not encouraged Miles's attentions to her! Now she had the uncomfortable feeling that he had some kind of hold over her. Where could he have found the locket? Was it possible that he knew of her visits to Maid's Hill and Moll Tyson's cottage? Then there was the conversation about witchcraft and the curious feeling of veiled threat she had felt. Just what did Miles intend to do?

She lay fully clothed on the bed, the coverlet pulled up to her chin—waiting and listening. Another half-hour and she must make a start on her journey to the cove. She was at least thankful for the Wilfords' early departure, though when she had left her uncle he had been in no mood for sleep. She could only hope that he had indulged himself with his favourite brandy before retiring.

Her thoughts turned to Roget who she would shortly see and as always her heart gave a little leap at the thought of him. Ever since their first meeting she had felt herself drawn to him and with each succeeding meeting the feeling had grown. Closing her eyes she pictured his strong, handsome face and the warm strength of his hands; she heard, in her

116

mind, his voice, a deep, manly voice which could be soft and soothing when he spoke to the children, or stern and resolute when he told of the horrors from which they had escaped. Deep in her heart a small voice spoke of love but she tried not to listen to it. He must surely look upon her as nothing more than a willing accomplice. He may be betrothed or even married in that other, secret life of his in which she played no part. And as for her—the day of her marriage to the unknown Philip Jefferson crept inexorably nearer. She sighed deeply. If only it could be different. If only there was some way she could control her own destiny.

Suddenly she stiffened and lay quite still as she heard the grandfather clock in the hall downstairs strike the half hour. It was time to start. Silently she slid over the edge of the bed and reached for her cloak. An ear to her uncle's door told her all she needed to know. His deep rhythmic snores vibrated the air and she gave a sigh of relief. Stealthily, she crept down the stairs and out to the kitchen.

It was a fine moonlit night and Abigail's heart lifted as she rode along the coast road with the salt breeze in her face. Tonight she was to play an even more daring part in the rescue. In her saddlebag she carried warmed milk for the infant as well as an extra shawl. Her heart beat faster with anticipation of what lay ahead.

Near the top of the cliff path was a group of gorse bush and here she found Roget's large chestnut horse tethered. She knew that Jed saw to this and she tied Bobby up alongside him then made her way carefully down the slippery path to the cove. As she came out among the jagged rocks at the bottom she stood quite still to listen. Above the gentle breaking of the waves upon the shore she heard the unmistakable dip and splash of oars. It seemed she was just in time. But on venturing out of the shelter of the rocks she caught her breath at what she saw. Not one boat, but two—Roget's near to the shore, the other, heading towards it from the headland. Her heart turned over as she saw Roget leap overboard, landing up to his waist in the water. Another man handed something to him and he began to wade ashore as fast as he could.

With a growing sense of urgency, Abigail ran towards him, feeling the waves wash over her feet, wetting the hem of her dress. Breathlessly he reached her and thrust the bundle into her arms.

'Quick—as fast as you can to the cottage,' he gasped. 'I'll draw their fire.'

'Who are they?' Abigail asked, watching the gap between the two boats closing with alarm.

'Excise men,' he said briefly. 'Quickly—I'll follow as soon as I can.'

The child held closely in her arms, Abigail scrambled back up the cliff path as fast as she could, her heart full of dread. If Roget had brought gold and jewellery with this child and the excise men caught him with it he would be in trouble. Suddenly a shot rang out and she froze in her tracks. They were firing! Dear God! she prayed. Oh dear God, let no harm come to him! Then she let out an involuntary cry as a hand closed over her shoulder.

'Don't be feared, Miss Abi—'tis only me— Bess. Dear Lord above, be they caught and taken?'

Faint with relief, Abigail clutched Bess's arm. Of course, she might have known the girl would be here to meet Jack. Her head had been so full of other thoughts she had overlooked the fact. 'Oh, Bess, it's the excise men. You must help me with the child. You can do no good here. Come—quickly.'

Bess paused to peer fearfully down to the beach but the boats were out of sight now under the overhang of the cliff. She turned to Abigail.

'Oh, Miss—my Jack. S'posin' he'm hurt *killed*?'

Abigail pulled at her sleeve. 'Come with me—you must. There's nothing we can do, but we must see that the child is safe. Bobby will take us both.'

The journey to Maid's Hill seemed interminable and Bess asked innumerable questions. Where were they going? Whose child was it? And what had Abigail to do with

119

it all? But the baby, a little boy of about a year old, woke and began to cry so that Abigail was too occupied to answer any of them.

At last they reached the sanctuary of the cottage and once inside Bess looked around her with awe, her eyes round as saucers.

'I never thought to see the inside o' this place! Oh, Miss Abi, do you s'pose Moll's ghost haunts it still? Be we safe 'ere?'

'Safer than out there or on the beach,' Abigail said wryly. 'Come, we have work to do. There is no time for such fancies.'

Bess took the child, attending to his needs while Abigail prepared the milk. Soon he slept again, held lovingly in Bess's arms while she crooned softly to him.

'Oh, Miss Abi, what a 'andsome little boy. I wish he was mine. When Jack'n me are married I wants lots o' babies.' She looked up at Abigail. 'But whose be 'e? Surely 'tis not babies Mr. Row-jay be smugglin'?'

'Yes, in a way it is, Bess,' Abigail told her. 'The children of people whose lives are in danger from the reign of terror across the sea in France. At this moment you are helping to save the life of the child you hold. He is one of the many who will return one day to make France a great and peaceful country once again.'

Bess's mouth dropped open as she gazed up at Abigail.

'You mean this is what my Jack've been

mixed up in these past months? And you'm part of it, too? But how?' she shook her head perplexedly. ' 'Tis beyond me.'

Briefly, Abigail explained her chance meeting with Roget and the way she had stumbled upon his secret work. Bess's eyes grew rounder and rounder as the story unfolded.

'And to think my Jack kept all this to 'iself all this time,' she breathed. 'You needn't be afeard, Miss Abi. I'll not tell a living soul. I wouldn't have harm come to the little 'ns for all the world.' She looked down tenderly at the sleeping child in her arms. 'Poor motherless little angel. May God punish them as done these wicked things!'

Abigail went to the window and lifted a corner of the curtain to peer out into the darkness anxiously. 'I do hope and pray that they are safe,' she whispered half to herself. She wondered how the excise men came to be in the cove tonight how they could have got wind of Roget's arrival. He had once said that there were spies everywhere, but who, here in Broomcott, could have betrayed him? And did it mean the end of his work? She turned to Bess.

'You had better take the child upstairs and put him to bed. Then I think you should get back to the Manor, Bess. If we should both be missed.'

Bess stood up. 'If you say so, Miss—though

I do wonder about my Jack.'

'I will find out what I can for you when Mr. Roget gets here,' Abigail promised, though even as she spoke anxiety gnawed at her. She wondered if she would see Roget tonight or indeed, ever again! And if he did not come what was she to do with the child? She watched as Bess ascended the staircase and presently heard her singing softly to the baby, then she moved to the table and began to pack the basket to occupy her trembling hands.

Outside the wind had freshened and she listened as it sang its weird lament—then suddenly she heard another sound and stiffened, every nerve strained. The next moment the door of the cottage burst open and Roget came in, closing it quickly behind him. Abigail stared at him. His clothes were soaked with sea water and his face was pallid and streaked with dirt. He pressed his right hand against the wall for support while he struggled to regain his breath, the other hung limply at his side. Then to her horror Abigail saw a dark stain spreading on the floor as blood dripped rapidly from his torn coat sleeve.

CHAPTER EIGHT

Her heart in her mouth she flew across the room to him. 'You're hurt! Oh, Roget, are you badly wounded? Is it a bullet?'

He put a hand on her shoulder. 'I think it is only a graze. I was lucky.' He smiled wryly. 'Another few inches and I would have been no more.'

She caught her breath. 'Oh, dear God! Come, sit down and let me look at it. You must rest. I am afraid you have lost a great deal of blood.'

When she had helped him to the seat by the fireplace she carefully removed his coat and tore away the blood-soaked shirt sleeve. He had been right, the bullet had not penetrated but had gouged deeply through the fleshy part of his upper arm, but the wound was clean. Without hesitation she tore a strip of linen from her petticoat and bathed the wound with some of the fresh water she always kept in the covered ewer on the hearth, then she bound it tightly to stem the bleeding. When it was done she brought him some of the milk from her basket.

'Drink this. And now you must rest or you will be faint from your wound.'

He shook his head. 'There is no time to be lost. I must take the child to Dorchester—to

Paul without delay.' For the first time he looked round the room. 'Where is he? Is he safe?'

Abigail nodded, remembering Bess. 'He is with my maid, Bess—No, please do not worry—' She pressed Roget back as he made to rise, his face concerned. 'She is a good, loyal girl and will help. She was waiting on the clifftop for Jack, her sweetheart, and there was nothing else for it but to enlist her help. She is caring for the child now, above.' She looked at him and passed a hand over his damp brow. 'You cannot ride to Dorchester tonight. You are not fit to go. It would not be safe, either for you or the child.'

He shook his head. 'There is nothing else for it. I *must* go.

'No!' She looked into his eyes. 'I *will*!'

He caught at her hand. 'No, Jenny! I could not allow it.

Her chin went up resolutely. 'Why not? No one would be suspicious of a *woman* with a baby—but a wounded man!' She stood up. 'Tell me how I am to recognize Paul and how I am to identify myself to him. When should I set out?'

'Jenny—wait! Give me time to think!' He reached out and took her hand, pulling her down on the settle beside him. Looking into her eyes he smiled ruefully. 'You quite take a man's breath away with your impulsiveness!' He took both of her hands into his, holding

124

them warmly. 'Have you considered the risks? If you were to be stopped.'

'If I were to be stopped' she interrupted. 'I should say that my name were Jenny Harding—that I am a sailor's wife and that I am travelling to Dorchester to stay with my mother while my man is away at sea.'

He smiled gently. 'Sailor's wives do not own horses and you cannot walk all the way. Besides, when I said 'stopped' I was thinking of the thieves and cut-purses who are always on the look-out for unprotected travellers.'

'I do not believe cut-purses would trouble to try to rob a poor woman with a child.' She placed her finger-tips over his lips as he opened them to protest again. 'Hush—it is settled. I will hear no more. When we have gone you can sleep on the bed upstairs. I will return in the morning with food and drink for you. Now—tell me how I will know Paul.'

For a moment he looked into her eyes, then, taking her by the shoulders he drew her to him and kissed her gently on the lips. 'You are a brave girl,' he said huskily. 'A brave, beautiful girl—but to let you do this—' But Abigail put up her hand to smooth the ruffled hair back from his brow. His kiss had disturbed her deeply and she knew without a doubt that she would risk anything, even death, for his sake— risk it gladly and joyfully.

'Roget' she whispered. 'There is so little time— Tell me quickly what I must do. By

125

noon tomorrow I will be here with you again—I promise.'

Something in her tone told him of her determination and he quickly told her where to meet the man known as 'Paul' and what she should say to make herself known to him.

'The dowry?' she asked. 'What is to be done with that?'

He shook his head. 'I hid it during my flight from the excise men. I dared not risk being caught with that and anyway, it would not be safe for you to carry valuables. I will retrieve it later when it is safe. You must explain this to Paul. He will understand.' He pulled off the heavy gold ring he wore on his little finger. 'Show him this as proof that you come from me—and you had better take my horse.' He slipped the ring on to her index finger, then, raising her hand to his lips, he pressed a kiss into the palm. 'God go with you, Jenny. Take great care, my dear.'

They looked into each other's eyes for a long moment and Roget's head bent slowly towards hers, but suddenly there was a movement on the stairs behind them and Abigail turned to see Bess descending. The girl looked uncertainly from one to the other.

'This is Bess, my maid,' Abigail said quickly. 'She has been caring for the baby. Bess—this is Mr. Roget.'

Bess blushed and dropped a quick curtsey, looking up anxiously into Roget's face. 'Oh, please sir—be my Jack safe? I been so mortal feared. An' please don't 'ee punish 'im, for 'e never told me nothing. I knew nought till tonight I swear it!'

Roget put a hand on her shoulder. 'Never fear, Bess. I do not doubt Jack's loyalty. And you can assure yourself that he is safe at home in his own bed at this moment.' He smiled wryly. 'I was the only one to give sport to the excise men.'

Bess blushed deeply, noticing his bandaged arm. 'Oh, sir. I'm dreadful sorry, I'm sure.'

'How did the excise men come to be in the cove tonight?' Abigail asked, voicing an earlier fear. 'Do you think someone could have betrayed you?'

But he shook his head. 'This coast abounds in smugglers. I have no doubt they thought we carried contraband.'

Abigail drew a sigh of relief as she turned to Bess. 'I am riding to Dorchester with the child,' she said. 'As you can see, Mr Roget is wounded and it would not be safe for him to go being weak from loss of blood. You are to go back to the—back home and if I am not back by breakfast time you must tell my uncle that I am ill and cannot rise. You had better go now.'

Bess gaped at her. 'Oh, Miss! But will you be safe? Should I go with'ee? What if—?'

But Abigail took the basket from the table and thrust it into her hands. 'Take Bobby. I am to take Mr. Roget's horse. I am sure I will be back in my room by breakfast time. Do not worry about me. No harm will come to me, I promise.'

When Bess had ridden off on Bobby, Abigail fetched the baby from the room upstairs. Taking the extra shawl she had brought with her she wrapped it tightly round herself and the child, tying the ends securely round her waist so as to leave her arms free, then she put on her cloak, pulling the hood over her head.

'Lock the door when I am gone,' she told Roget. 'When I return I shall knock three times—thus—' She tapped twice sharply on the door, then knocked loudly once. 'Go up now and try to sleep. Do not concern yourself for me. I shall be quite safe.'

He rose and came with her to the door, cupping her chin in his hand he looked deep into her eyes. 'My heart goes with you, Jenny,' he said softly.

Her eyes shone. 'Then I shall have nothing to fear,' she whispered.

Dawn was breaking as she walked wearily into the town of Dorchester. The ride, though uneventful, had been tiring and slow, hampered as she was with the child who had been restless and fretful and now her shoulders ached with his weight. She had tied up her mount a short distance from the town in a secluded place, wishing to make as little noise as possible.

She was to look for the man known as 'Paul' at the King's Head Inn and she was thankful that she knew the inn's whereabouts for there was no one of whom she could ask the way.

The inn yard was deserted and she stood for a moment in the shadows, wondering whether to venture inside. The baby was hungry and she herself was chilled and sorely in need of refreshment, but she had brought no money with her with which to buy food and drink. As she was wondering what course to take she heard a church clock strike four and remembered that this was the hour at which Paul was to arrive. She was about to move off and take a look down the road when the clatter of hooves heralded the arrival of a traveller and she drew back into the shadows again. A post-chaise drew into the yard and an ostler ran forward from the stables to attend to the horses. As she watched, a tall, grey-haired man stepped down from the chaise. He wore a blue coat and walked with a stoop and, when he turned in her direction to give instructions to the driver she saw that he had a lean, kindly face—just as Roget had described to her. Taking her courage in both hands she stepped forward out of the shadows before he could enter the inn.

'Forgive me, sir—' She touched his sleeve. 'Have I the honour of addressing 'Paul'?'

He turned to look at her, his face bemused,

but at that moment the child held closely against her let out a wail. He stepped back in alarm, then leaned forward to peer into her face, half hidden by the hood of her cloak.

'Who are you?'

'I am known as 'Jenny',' she said quietly. 'I have come from 'Roget' who is indisposed. I am to deliver the—package you are expecting.' She drew back her cloak to reveal the child and at the same time, held out the hand that bore Roget's ring.'

The man seemed to take in the situation at once and taking her arm he drew her towards the inn. 'Come with me, my dear,' he said. 'You and the child shall eat while you tell me what has befallen my friend.'

A bright fire burned in the hearth of the dining-room which was occupied only by one or two sleepy travellers who had risen to make an early start to their journey. After being fed with a bowl of gruel the baby went back to sleep and Abigail made him comfortable on a chair beside her while she eagerly applied herself to the mug of mulled ale and plate of beef which the serving girl had set before her.

Paul watched her quizzically for a moment. She was no serving wench or country girl, that much was plain from her speech, so who was she to have the courage to make this journey alone? What connection had she with Roget and where was he? When she had satisfied her hunger he voiced these questions and Abigail told him briefly what had taken place and of her part in the exploit, ending by assuring him of Roget's safety and that of the 'dowry'.

He nodded. 'I see that we have found a useful ally my dear, though why you should take grave risks to help us I cannot see.'

Her eyes looked into his. 'My father died for France, sir,' she said simply. 'It is little enough that I do.'

He pressed her hand. 'I am sorry, my dear, very sorry indeed. But now, if you are rested, I think you must be on your way before the day is upon us.'

She rose, giving the sleeping child a last wistful look. 'Will he—will he be well-cared for, sir?' she asked.

He smiled. 'Perhaps I should not divulge the fact—but being of such tender age this child is to be cared for by my own daughter.' He stood up. 'Go now, child. Safe journey and may God bless you for your courage.'

The sky was pearly pink as she walked the short distance to where she had left Roget's horse tethered. Once in the saddle she urged him forward, riding as fast as she could. If she were to preside over her uncle's breakfast table she would need the speed of the wind itself!

Jed was in the stable yard when she rode in. Her hair was tangled by the wind and her cheeks whipped to a fresh rosy pink. Her

131

mount's glossy flanks were flecked with sweat and his belly heaved with exhaustion. Jed asked no questions but seized the bridle.

'Get you inside, Miss,' he said in a low voice. 'I'll see to 'un.'

She slid stiffly down from the saddle. 'Where will you put him, Jed?' she asked. 'I am afraid I have ridden him sorely. He is much in need of attention, poor creature.'

'He'll get it, never you fear, Miss. Just get inside before you'm seen. 'Tis close on six o'clock.'

Like a ghost she slipped in through the buttery—past Sarah's broad back as she leaned over the fire in the kitchen and up the stairs to her room, closing the door behind her with a sigh. She looked longingly at the bed. If only she could crawl into it and sleep her tiredness away. Her bones ached unbearably and her eyes felt as though they were full of sand. She yawned widely. Was it really only last night —a few short hours ago, that the Wilfords had come to dine?

The door opened and Bess slipped in, carrying a heavy can of hot water. 'I heard you creep up, Miss Abi, and I reckoned you'd be glad of a good hot wash.' She put the can down and threw her arms round her mistress. 'Oh, I'm *that* glad to see you, Miss Abi! I've been fair mazed wi' worry. Was it all right? Did you hand the little 'un over safe like?'

Abigail peeled her clothes off gratefully and

washed her aching limbs with the comforting hot water, telling Bess as she did so of her journey and the child's safe delivery.

Dressed in clean clothes and with her hair brushed and smoothed into place she felt better, but she confessed her anxiety for Roget at Moll's cottage.

'I hope he is rested and that he has not taken a fever, Bess.' Her brow furrowed. 'He looked so pale and his wound was very deep. He must have lost a great deal of blood. '

Bess smiled. 'He be a fine big strong man, Miss Abi.

I'm sure you've no need to worry yourself about 'im—except o'course if 'n you'm more than a friend to 'im.' She bit her lip and looked sideways at her mistress, noting with satisfaction that her colour had risen. 'Not that I could blame 'ee for bein' sweet on 'im,' she added. 'Andsome as they come, 'e is.' She giggled. 'And if I 'adn't come down them stairs when I did last night I reckon you'd 'a got a kiss off 'n 'im!'

'How dare you say such a thing, you impertinent girl!' Abigail slapped the girl's arm soundly, but Bess only laughed.

'Why so angry, Miss Abi? I'd 'a thought you'd be proud to love a man like that! An'im lovin' you too—looking' at you wi' them 'andsome eyes o' his full o' moonshine.'

Abigail stared at her, her assumed indignation quite forgotten. 'Oh, Bess, you're

133

right —I do love him. But what use is it?' She sat down heavily on the edge of the bed. 'My uncle has me betrothed to his odious stepson and it seems there is no escape.'

Bess's eyes softened. 'You could run away, Miss—elope.'

Abigail sighed. 'It's useless. For all I know Roget may be betrothed himself, or even married.'

When she went down to breakfast Abigail found that her uncle's temper had not improved with sleep. His difference of opinion with Parson Wilford had left its mark on him and added to that he had received two communications from the post-boy which seemed to have disturbed him. He glared at her across the table.

'It appears we are to have guests, niece.' He waved the letters at her. 'I have had word from an old acquaintance of mine from across the sea. A countryman of your father's— Monsieur Claude Dupont. He is to pay us a visit.'

Abigail's heart leapt. 'From France, Uncle? He is coming here from France? Perhaps he knew Papa. Perhaps he can tell me—'

But Thomas cut her short. 'No, child. He has not lived in France for some time—for which, no doubt, he is thankful. Though it may amuse him to hear you jabber to him in his native language, I daresay.' He picked up the other letter which lay before him. 'You will
134

also be interested to know that we are to expect the long-awaited visitation from my stepson, Philip.' He looked at her. 'It is quite opportune I shall have business to discuss with Monsieur Dupont and while I do so you can make yourself acquainted with your betrothed. There will be two rooms to prepare, for both of our guests are expected tomorrow afternoon. You had better get Sarah and the girl to attend to it.' He looked up at her impatiently. 'Well' he thundered. 'What the devil are you gaping at, girl? Have I said something outrageous?'

Abigail felt as though her heart had stopped beating. So she was to meet Philip Jefferson at last and just when she knew beyond the shadow of a doubt that she could love no other man but Roget. How could she bring herself to face him—make herself agreeable to him? How could she contemplate the thought of marriage with him? At her uncle's bellow she dragged her thoughts back to the task he had spoken of.

'Y—yes, of course, Uncle. It shall be attended to directly after breakfast. Two rooms, you said. Is there anything else you wish me to do?'

He peered at her suspiciously. He had expected more protestations and impudence. But now that he came to look at her she did not seem herself. There were dark smudges under her eyes and although she answered him meekly enough her thoughts seemed to be elsewhere. He sincerely hoped she was not ailing. He could not abide ailing women, especially under his own roof. The fees these sawbones fellows demanded were nothing short of outrageous!

'What is the matter with you, girl? Are you unwell?' he barked.

'Unwell? No. I—I am in excellent health, Uncle,' she stammered. 'It is just just that it is not every day that one faces the prospect of meeting the man one is to marry.'

Thomas snorted derisively. 'Huh! I trust you are not about to have an attack of the vapours! I cannot see why you females throw yourselves into such a case over marriage. When all is said and done it is merely a change of status. Good God, girl—you *wish* to be a wife and mother, do you not? You *wish* to fulfil your destiny as a woman?'

Abigail's eyes flashed with anger as she looked at her uncle's exasperated purple face. 'Indeed, I do, Uncle,' she said, her voice carefully controlled. 'But I would rather have chosen the time and the man myself.'

'Pah!' Thomas's complexion deepened from purple to puce as he rose and began to pace the room. 'What can you know, girl, of men and the ways of the world? Where is your gratitude? I have taken you from the nunnery where you were left to rot and arranged a good match for you. If it were not for my generosity you would be destitute!—forced to work as a servant or a governess. Let me hear no more of your ungrateful talk! When my stepson comes you will make yourself agreeable to him, do you hear?' He bent to glare into her face. 'And do not entertain thoughts of making yourself unattractive so as to repulse him—for I would not put it past you!'

Abigail stood slowly to face him, her cheeks deathly pale and her hands trembling as she clutched the edge of the table.

'It would be less hard, Uncle, if I knew what your true intentions for me were. Although betrothed unwillingly to Mr. Jefferson you instructed me to make myself agreeable to Miles Wilford. Now, it seems, the position is reversed. Am I to be used as a pawn in some game for your gain? If this is so I would prefer some honest labour such as you describe.'

For a long moment Thomas stood spluttering helplessly at her. So astounded was he at her cool effrontery that his anger stuck fast in his chest. Although she was confoundedly impudent he had to admit that the girl had spirit. Finally he picked up his riding crop from the table and slapped it against his leg.

'Dammit girl, you *will* do as I say! How dare you question my choice for you? Get about your duties. There will be no more discussions on the matter.' And with that he strode from the room.

Abigail stared at the door as it slammed behind her uncle's bristling back. Despair washed over her in a wave that overwhelmed her and she laid her head dejectedly on her arms, tears squeezing themselves out from her closed eyelids.

'Miss Abi—be you all right?' Bess crept quietly into the room and stood looking helplessly at her mistress. 'I 'eard the master a 'shoutin',' she continued. 'An' then 'e stormed out o' the 'ouse like thunder. Oh, Miss'—she touched Abigail's arm. 'Don't 'ee weep. Is there ought I can do?'

Abigail sat up, brushing the tears from her cheeks. 'Philip Jefferson is coming. He arrives tomorrow. Oh, Bess—if I were only sure that Roget loved and wanted me I would run away with him this very day. I would do anything rather than marry as my uncle intends.'

Bess stroked her mistress's thick wavy hair thoughtfully. 'You haven't forgotten that you're to take 'im food this mornin', 'ave you, Miss? You could talk to 'im—tell 'im all an' see what 'e do say. 'Tis my guess he'll not let another man 'ave 'ee.'

Abigail blushed as she looked at Bess. 'I—I could not,' she protested. 'It may be that you are mistaken and that all he feels for me is—is comradeship. I dare not reveal my heart to him.'

Bess shrugged. 'Then you mun lose 'im. Oh, believe me, Miss Abi—he *do* love 'ee. I'd stake

138

my life on't. If you don't speak to 'un you'll maybe not get another chance. Come on now. I've packed a basket ready wi' some o' the fine fare left over from last night's dinner. Will 'ee take it to 'un now?'

Abigail rose eagerly from the table, her heart quickening, then she remembered that there were rooms to be made ready for their guests. 'Oh, Bess—there is work to be done first,' she said. 'Rooms to be cleaned and aired and beds to be made.'

But Bess shook her head impatiently. 'I can do that, Miss. I'll do it right, never fear. Now, you make yourself pretty and be away to Maid's Hill.'

It was risky, being seen going to Maid's Hill with a basket of food in broad daylight and Abigail kept to the shelter of the hedges, hoping she would meet no one on her way. Once out on the open Dorchester road, however, she urged Bobby forward, her heart quickening at the prospect of seeing Roget.

Securing the little cob in his accustomed place she made her way up the hill and gave two sharp taps and one loud one on the door. After a pause it was opened to her and she found herself inside standing face to face with Roget. He looked better. The colour had returned to his cheeks and he had washed and tidied himself the best he could, though there was a dark growth of stubble on his cheeks.

His eyes lit up as he smiled down at her.

'Jenny! Thank God you're safe. Tell me, did all go well?'

She nodded, going to the table and beginning to unpack the basket. 'I encountered no trouble at all. It was child's play,' she said lightly. 'But you must be hungry. I have food, and see—' She held out a rolled towel containing a razor which Bess had thoughtfully included. 'Bess has thought of everything for your comfort.'

After he had shaved and eaten Abigail dressed his wound and was relieved to see that it was clean and dry, showing no signs of infection.

'I must leave here as soon as it is dark,' he told her urgently. 'Where is my horse?'

'He is being attended to,' she told him. 'I will see that he is here for you at nightfall.' She touched his arm. 'But do take care. It would be a pity to open the wound again when it is healing so well. You should rest the arm.'

He smiled down at her. 'I will try to. I do not know what I would have done without you last night, Jenny. I have been so worried for your safety. I could not have forgiven myself if anything had happened to you.'

As she looked up into his eyes a great surge of feeling went through her and she reached for his hands, gripping them warmly.

'Knowing that gives me a charmed life,' she said. 'I feel that nothing can harm me as long as I am in your thoughts.'

He drew her to him, folding his arms closely round her till she could feel his heart beating against her own, then, bending his head he found her lips and kissed her. Her arms crept round him and she clung to him, her heart singing like a bird. He *did* love her—just as she loved him.

At last he released her and looked down into her eyes apologetically. 'Forgive me, Jenny. It is ungallant of me to take advantage of our being alone like this. But two people cannot endure what we have been through together without feeling a certain—affinity.'

She laughed and shook her head. 'Why, Roget! You are so formal and polite. I liked you better as you were before. Will you please kiss me again?'

His face broke into a delighted smile and he pulled her again into his arms, kissing her lips, her eyelids and her forehead, murmuring little words of endearment between kisses till she was quite breathless and pushed him gently away.

'Roget! Oh, my love would you have me lose my breath altogether?' She laughed gently and, reaching up she took his face between her hands. 'I love you,' she said, her voice trembling. 'I love you more than I have ever loved anyone in my whole life—more than I love my life. I want to go with you when you go tonight. Say you will take me with you, my darling.'

He looked at her for a long moment, biting his lip, then he drew her close and kissed her deeply. As he put her from him she saw that his face was clouded and there was pain in his voice as he said:

'I cannot take you, Jenny. It is out of the question.' He turned from her and she stood for a moment, staring at him incredulously. 'You—you do not love me, then?' She said at last.

He drew a deep breath. 'Do not say that. Of course I love you. You cannot doubt it.'

She ran to him, her hands on his shoulders, pulling him round to face her. 'Then you must take me—you must. It is the only chance we have. Tomorrow will be too late!'

He frowned, shaking his head. 'How can I make you understand, my love? I cannot explain—but I cannot take you with me tonight. I have a—a mission to complete.'

'Take me with you,' she begged.

'Darling—it is impossible.' He lifted his hands helplessly.

She threw herself against him, her arms tightly round his waist. 'Oh, Roget do not say it. Do not send me away, I beg you. I want to be with you for ever, my love. I want to belong to you—to be your wife—to—to bear your children.'

He raised her face to his, one finger beneath her chin, and gently brushed away the tears that ran down her cheeks.

'You should never bare your heart to any man like that, my darling,' he said, his voice heavy with emotion. 'But I want you to know that I am proud to hear you say those words to me. You must know that I want these things too—so much that I can hardly bear the pain of wanting them. But there are reasons why it cannot be—at least for a while.'

She looked up at him, her brown eyes fearful and brimming with tears. 'There is—someone else? You are betrothed to another?' Almost imperceptively, he nodded and she swallowed back her tears. 'I *also* am betrothed,' she told him vehemently. 'To a man I do not and can never love. But if we were to run away tonight—' He stopped her words with a kiss so passionate that her whole being was weak with longing. Then, as she buried her head against his shoulder he said quietly:

'Please—I beg you to trust me, my dearest. What you want cannot be. But we will be together some day, that I will promise you.'

She stared up at him in disbelief, then, pushing him from her she took a step backwards, shaking her head.

'You *cannot* love me!' she cried. 'If you did you could not be so cruel! If we do not leave here tonight I shall wed my betrothed and we shall never meet again.' She picked up her cloak and basket, then turned to him, her mouth tremulous. 'I will see to it that your horse is ready and waiting for you at nightfall. Goodbye, Roget!'

'Jenny—wait!' He took a step towards her, his hand outstretched, but she was gone, whisking through the door with a flurry of skirts and running down the hill to Bobby. Then, blinded by tears she was off, along the road and across the fields, not caring now who saw her—her throat constricted with sobs and her heart torn in two.

When she reached the gate of the stable yard she was exhausted with fatigue and emotion. She dismounted and was leading Bobby to his stable, her head down and deep in thought when she almost ran into Danny, the skip-jack who was crossing the yard with a heavy milk can. She looked up at him in surprise.

'Oh, Danny. Have you been to Mary Bray's with the goat's milk? How is little Matty?'

The boy's face was troubled as he looked up at her and he took a step backwards. 'She—she won't have the milk no more, Miss,' he mumbled. 'Said I weren't to take it.'

Abigail frowned. 'But it is important that she keep drinking it, does she wish me to take another look at the child?' She broke off, looking curiously at the boy. His face had turned pale and he was edging away from her along the wall. She grasped his arm. 'Danny! What is the matter? Are you ill?'

He shook his head vigorously. 'No, Miss, I

144

baint ill—I don't want no cures!'

Somewhere deep in Abigail's mind a warning bell sounded. She held tightly to the boy's collar. 'What are they saying, Danny? Tell me at once!' But his white face with its round frightened eyes stared back dumbly at her. She shook him impatiently. 'Don't be so foolish, boy. Have I ever hurt you? Nothing bad will happen to you but you must tell me what is being said!'

Danny's mouth opened and shut several times before he could get any words out and when he did she felt her heart plummet. Her worst fears were confirmed.

'They'm—they'm sayin' the milk is Devil's milk,' he said in a hushed whisper. 'An' that babes who drinks it will turn into Devil's children. They'm sayin' it's you a'doin' his wicked works, Miss—collectin' babes for the evil one. They'm sayin' you'm a—a *witch*!'

CHAPTER NINE

Bess sang a snatch of a hymn tune as she came out into the garden with her basket of washing. She loved music, it was what she enjoyed most about church on Sunday evenings and so taken was she with the sound of her own voice and the task in hand that she did not at first realize that she was not alone in the garden. It was

145

only when she turned to drape a pillow-slip over a currant bush that she was aware that someone was in the arbour.

Jed had helped Abigail to build the arbour. There had been one in the garden of a French chateau she had once visited with her papa when she was a little girl and she had never forgotten it. It was built in the shelter of the garden's west wall, sheltered from the sea winds but now the profusion of pink and white roses that grew over it almost hid from view the little seat inside. Bess caught only a glimpse of spotted muslin but it was enough to tell her who was there. She gave a last tweak to the pillow-slip and made her way across the grass.

'Miss Abi! Why, I thought you was up to Maid's Hill.' She stopped as she caught sight of Abigail's stricken face. 'Oh, Miss! Be you all right? It's not Mr. Row-jay? He baint worse?'

Abigail shook her head. 'No, Bess. His wound is healing well—but Oh, *Bess*!' The tears in her eyes overflowed and ran helplessly down her cheeks. Bess went to her and gathered her into her arms, murmuring softly: 'There now, my pretty, don't 'ee fret so. What be wrong? Tell Bess—Bess'll make it all right again.'

'Oh, Bess, you can't! There is nothing to be done—*nothing*!' She laid her head against the girl's bosom and sobbed.

'I—I have lost Roget. Sent him away—for

ever. I may never see him again!'

Bess let her cry her tears out, rocking her to and fro and comforting her as she would a child. Then, when the sobs abated a little she lifted the corner of her apron and gently wiped the tears from her mistress's face. 'Now then, Miss Abi,' she said calmly. 'Do'ee tell Bess what've'appened an' we'll see what's to be done about it.'

Abigail swallowed hard. 'I—I told him of my feelings, Bess. I would not have done, only something happened which made me think he shared them. Once I began though, I seemed unable to stop and I said—Oh, Bess—when I think of what I said I go hot with shame. He— he said he could not take me with him. It seems it is as I thought he is betrothed to another.'

Bess shrugged. 'But did you find out 'ow 'e *felt*, Miss? Did 'e say 'e *loved* 'ee?'

Abigail sighed. 'He did—but I fear it was only to save my pride. I was so angry with myself and so beset that I—I told him I would marry my betrothed and never—never see him again. Oh, Bess!' Fresh tears slid down her cheeks.

Bess shook her impatiently. 'There now, don't take on so. T'was only a lovers' tiff, to be sure. I'd like a penny for every time I've told my Jack I didn't want to see 'un no more!'

But Abigail grasped her arm. 'There is something else, Bess. When I got back I met

Danny in the yard. He had been to take Mary Bray her goat's milk but she sent him back with it. They are saying in the village that I am in league with the Devil—that I am a witch! Oh, Bess, whatever shall I do?'

Bess's mouth dropped open and the colour drained from her face. 'Oh, my dear Lord! But 'ow could they think such things when you'm been so good and kind to 'em? 'Tis wicked and cruel!'

Abigail shook her head. 'Miles and Rebecca Wilford warned me that something of the sort might happen last night, but I took no notice of them. Like you, Bess, I thought the village folk were my friends. It seems it was the goat's milk that set them against me.'

Bess's eyes narrowed. 'The Wilfords, eh?' Her lips compressed. 'They two are no friends o' you'n, Miss Abi, you take my word on't. I'd stake my life on't it's they who are at the bottom o' this.' She slipped a protective arm round Abigail's shoulders again. 'Don't 'ee worry now. Bess'll put a word in for 'ee in the village. When I be done they'll be ashamed o' their—selves.' She looked into her mistress's pale face. 'You be fair mazed wi' tiredness. Not a wink did 'ee get last night. You go up to your room and sleep awhile. Things do always look better when you'm rested. Then afterwards you can go back up to Maid's Hill an' make peace with Mr. Row-jay.'

Abigail sighed wearily. 'You're right, Bess. I

148

do long to sleep—but go back to Maid's Hill? No! I could never face Roget again, not after what I said.'

But later, when she awoke refreshed after several hours exhausted sleep, she found her thoughts had cleared. The afternoon sun streamed through the casement and she lay stretching her refreshed limbs and thinking over what she should do. The first thing was to seek out Jed and tell him to have Roget's horse ready at Maid's Hill at nightfall. Then she had the idea: she would send him a letter. Of course! Why had she not thought of it before?

Throwing back the covers she got out of bed and dressed quickly, then running down to her uncle's study she found paper and quill and began to write. It was more difficult than she had foreseen and she made several attempts before she was satisfied. In the end she confined herself to the simplest of messages, which read:

'Dear Roget, Forgive me for my outburst this morning. I behaved in a foolish, childish manner and I am ashamed. I shall be ready to assist you with the next 'cargo' and promise not to speak to you so foolishly again. Your sincere friend—Jenny.'

Reading it through she sanded it carefully, folded and sealed it, then went in search of Jed. She found him in the stable yard and Bess with him. When she saw her mistress coming towards her looking rested and so much better her homely face beamed.

'There now! You do look more like yourself now, Miss Abi. I'll go and make'ee something to eat'n drink.' As she passed Abigail she laid a hand on her arm and lowered her voice. 'I been to the village, Miss. I talked to Mary Bray an' some o' the others. Don't 'ee fret, Miss. They'm not against 'ee. 'Tis what I said—someone've been fillin' their 'eads wi' rubbishy tales. But I put 'un right on't, don't 'ee fear.'

She bustled indoors and, feeling relieved, Abigail gave Roget's instruction to Jed, handing him also the letter she had written. He promised to attend to it and she went back into the kitchen to find Sarah in a bad mood, resentful at being left with the preparations for Thomas Hargreaves' guests alone. She eyed Abigail with a sour expression.

'I do 'ope you'm quite recovered, Miss—from your—*indisposition*,' she said with heavy sarcasm. 'And now that Bess've done your errands in the village mebbe I can 'ave 'er to 'elp me get them rooms ready.' She jerked her head ceilingwards. 'Mr. Philip 'asn't been 'ere for many a long month—must be nigh on a year or more. The beds'll need a proper airin' ' She put her hands on her hips. 'An' another thing—will this 'ere foreign gentleman be wantin' special food—an' if so will *you* be takin' on the cookin' of it—because I baint no 'and at outlandish foreign muck as you are!'

150

Abigail almost laughed. It was as much as Sarah could do to make a rabbit stew, let alone prepare French cuisine. She shook her head.

'My uncle tells me that Monsieur Dupont has lived for many years in this country. No doubt he will be accustomed to our food by now.' She lifted her chin and looked the housekeeper coolly in the eye. 'I am sorry, Sarah, if you feel that too great a burden is being placed upon you. Bess will help me to prepare the rooms now if you will get on with cooking dinner. I wonder if you feel you are growing too old for the work here? Perhaps I should speak to my uncle about engaging a younger and more able worker. '

The two women stared at each other for several seconds, Abigail's eyes clear and direct, while Sarah's, at first defiant, slid away uncertainly, looking down at her fingers which she twisted together.

'N—no, Miss Abigail—don't do that,' she said in a humbler tone. 'It do be a lot for one to manage to be sure—but I'm not complainin'.'

Abigail nodded. 'I am glad, Sarah. For there is no room for complaining servants at the Manor. There are a great many women in the village who would be only too glad of your job.' And so saying she turned to Bess. 'Fetch the warming-pans, Bess, and the clean linen, We have work to do.'

Once out of Sarah's hearing on the back

stairs, Bess spluttered and giggled. 'That were tellin' 'er, Miss Abi, an' no mistake. Oh my dear Lord—'er *face*! No one baint never spoken to 'er like you do. She can't get over it!'

Back in the kitchen Sarah muttered to herself as she bent over the fire, replacing the coals taken off to fill the warming-pans.

'Hoity-toity piece!' she growled. 'Wait till they'm wed 'ee to Mr. Gad-about Philip. Your pretty feet'll dance to 'is tune then—an' serves 'ee right!'

Sunday morning dawned bright and clear. From her window Abigail could smell the fresh tang of the sea and the sun was warm and caressing on her face, but her heart gave no answering lift. This day she would meet Philip Jefferson. This was the day that her fate could be sealed, perhaps irrevocably. The only comfort she had was that she had at least made her peace with Roget. Perhaps after reading her letter he would not think quite so badly of her.

Over breakfast her uncle informed her that he would not be accompanying her to church this morning and she felt her heart sink. Normally she would have been relieved to have been free of his company but being the first time she would mingle with the village folk after the spreading of the ugly rumours, she would have been glad even of his support. Despite Bess's protests on her behalf she could not help but feel apprehensive. No one would dare behave disrespectfully of her in her uncle's presence—but alone.

She looked up. 'May I also remain at home this morning, Uncle?' she asked.

Thomas glowered at her. 'Certainly not! After what passed last night between the Reverend Wilford and myself he might think I were piqued if neither of us appeared. I would not give him that satisfaction! Monsieur Dupont and I have business to talk over and there are papers I must prepare. You will go alone, girl.'

Abigail frowned. 'Business, Uncle? What could Monsieur Dupont possibly have to do with the Manor?'

Thomas threw down his knife and fork with a clatter and his furious bloodshot glare silenced her before she could say more. 'How dare you question my private affairs, girl? Women and business do not mix; the female brain is not equipped for such things. Before you leave for church you will see to it that Sarah knows what to prepare for the day's meals. Oh—and the brougham will not be at your disposal today. I am sending Harker to Dorchester with it to meet Monsieur Dupont off the London coach. My stepson, I am given to understand, will travel by horseback.'

Abigail, who had by now reached the door, turned and eyed her uncle coldly. 'I see, Uncle—you will not be sending a farm cart to meet Monsieur Dupont then, as you did me?'

Thomas spluttered. 'Farm cart! Of course not, girl! Monsieur Dupont is a cultured gentleman, not a chit of a girl!'

As she closed the door behind her, Abigail wondered, not for the first time, how Emma Jefferson, her uncle's late wife, had borne his arrogance and chauvinism.

The walk to church was not unpleasant along the leafy sunlit lanes. Abigail wore a gown of pale yellow lawn with a broad silk sash striped in gold and green. Her straw hat was trimmed with green and yellow ribbons and with her dark curls bouncing on her shoulders she made a pretty sight. She was almost within sight of the little church of St. Catherine's when a carriage drew up beside her and she heard the window being lowered. Turning, she saw Rebecca Wilford's heavy face looking out at her.

'Why, Abigail! Do you *walk* to church?'

Abigail smiled. 'The brougham has gone to Dorchester to meet a guest of my uncle's from the London coach, but I do not mind. It is such a pleasant morning.'

Rebecca clucked disapprovingly. 'But that is hardly the point, my dear Abigail. For the Squire's niece to be seen *walking* to church! Indeed I cannot allow such a scandal.' She opened the carriage door. 'Do *please* get in—I insist.'

Reluctantly, Abigail did as she was asked but immediately regretted it when she found

154

that Miles also occupied the carriage. He smiled, making room for her on the seat beside him and pressing his thigh against hers.

'How very delightful you look, Abigail,' he drawled. 'The very epitome of a summer's morning, is she not, sister?'

Rebecca's eyes had not failed to take in Abigail's appearance. She herself wore an elaborate gown of plum-coloured silk, its colour doing nothing to enhance her pallid complexion and red hair, and the abundance of frills, bows and laces making her already bulky form seem even bulkier. 'Why was it?' she asked herself furiously, 'that this wretched girl could look cool and elegant in a gown that must surely have cost but a fraction of the one she herself wore?' She pursed her lips into a smile.

'You really must tell me, Abigail dear, how you manage to achieve that simple, countrified look in such a sweet way. It is positively *rustic*. Such a novelty!' She leaned forward. 'I have heard that Philip Jefferson is expected at the Manor today. Perhaps you will tell him that I will call on him to invite him to dine at the Parsonage. I must also circulate the news that he is at home. The poor man will miss the social whirl and be dreadfully bored if he is to be here long.'

'I think not.' Abigail moved along the seat, as far away from Miles and his oppressive closeness as she could. 'The main purpose for his visit on this occasion is his betrothal—to me.'

However unhappy the prospect of her betrothal to Philip Jefferson made her, Abigail could not help but be amused at the effect her announcement had on the two Wilfords. There was a stunned silence in the carriage as they stared, first at her, then at each other, but there was no time for them to voice their thoughts on the matter for at that moment the carriage came to a halt outside the church gate.

Abigail was the only occupant of the Hargreaves family pew and she felt that every pair of eyes in the congregation were upon her. As the service progressed she saw, out of the corner of her eye, that earnest consultations were taking place between Miles and Rebecca and just before his father mounted the pulpit to begin his sermon, Miles discreetly left by the side door.

When the service came to a close Abigail walked out into the pleasant freshness of the churchyard. The gravestones were dappled with moving leafy patterns of light and shade and she lingered a while, nodding and passing the time of day with those she knew among the congregation. She was relieved to find there was no coldness or suspicion among them, even Mary Bray came up to her and asked to be forgiven for sending the milk back. Abigail drew a sigh of relief. It seemed Bess had laid all doubts about her good intentions to rest.

As she reached the lych-gate the Reverend Wilford extended a plump hand towards her.

'I hope I find you well this pleasant morning, Miss Abigail,' he beamed. 'And your uncle—I hope he is—er—well.'

She nodded. 'Quite well, thank you. He is expecting a visit today from a business acquaintance and wished to prepare for his arrival.'

The Reverend Wilford nodded, smiling benignly. 'Quite so—quite so. I knew there must be a sound reason for his absence. He is one of the staunchest members of my flock—as indeed the Squire should be.'

Abigail's lips twitched as she took her leave. She would dearly have liked to see her uncle's reaction to being termed a member of the Reverend Wilford's 'flock'.

Out in the lane it was quiet. The congregation had melted away in the direction of the village and there were few who went Abigail's way, towards the sea. She was relieved to find that the young Wilfords had departed. It must be quite in order, she mused, to be seen walking from church! She had just reached the bend in the lane when a small boy scrambled to his feet from where he had been sitting in the grass. As he came forward Abigail recognized him as Toby, one of Mary Bray's older children. He ran up to her.

'Miss—oh, Miss!'

She stopped. 'Why Toby, is something wrong?'

He swallowed, red in the face. 'There be a traveller hurt, Miss—up to Maid's Hill. He bade me fetch you. You'm to go quick, Miss.'

Abigail's heart turned over. Roget! It must be he! His wound must have worsened, preventing him from leaving last night. 'It's all right, Toby,' she said breathlessly. 'You did well to give me the message. I'll go at once.'

He ran off and she stood there for a moment wondering what was best to do. At last she decided it would be quickest to walk. If she went back to the Manor for Bobby she might be delayed and while she was walking there she could be at Maid's Hill.

Her dainty kid shoes were soon muddied by the soft earth of the fields she crossed and the hem of her gown sullied but she paid no heed to them. Roget needed her. He had sent for her and her only thoughts were for him.

She was out of breath by the time she reached Maid's Hill and paused to rest for a moment before beginning to climb it. As she emerged from the copse of trees where she usually tethered Bobby she saw the 'Dancing Maids' standing jagged against the sky, their edges touched with silver from the sunlight— then all at once it was as though some strange magic were taking place. Over the top of each of the stones a face appeared. She stopped in her tracks and stared as bodies followed the

158

faces and she was faced by a ring of young men, their faces lit with some strange excitement. Suddenly there came a blood-curdling whoop:

'She's 'ere! The witch 'as come!'

And a moment later the air was full of flying missiles. A stone hit her on the shoulder with a stinging smack and a clod of earth burst against her back as she turned and began to run back down the hill. She headed for the shelter of the trees but they were too quick for her; they came whooping down the hillside and a moment later her feet skidded to a halt as she found herself surrounded.

She stood rooted to the spot, feeling like a hunted animal, the grinning faces of the mob on every side. There seemed to be about a dozen of them, large lusty young men, none of whom she had ever seen before. She looked round fearfully at their faces, they looked triumphant—breathless and eager as they waited like hunters for the kill. In a desperate effort she appealed to them, her voice shaking:

'Please—you are making a mistake. I am not a witch—I have only sought to heal—the little ones and the old and sick.' But she stopped in mid—sentence as the truth dawned on her. They cared nothing whether she were a witch or not. They were drunk and out for sport. Her hand flew to her breast as they began to close in on her, their circle growing smaller as they closed the gaps. One of them gave her a

159

push and she fell heavily against the man in front of her. He laughed and pushed her back. Soon she was hurtling from one to the other like a ball in a game; spun, turned and twisted; her gown torn where they snatched at her, her hair loosened and tangled as their hands grabbed at it. Finally she fell dizzily to the ground and lay there looking up terrified into their frantic, excited faces.

'Well, lads—what'll we do wi'er?' one of them yelled. 'Carry 'er down t'the pond an' give 'un a duckin'?'

'No!' The largest of them pushed the others aside and stood over her, leering down sadistically. 'Time enough for that. There be other sport t'be 'ad wi' er first!'

A shout of raucous laughter went up as they roared their approval and Abigail covered her face with her hands. But as her lips moved in a silent prayer a voice rang out, making her look up. The crowd had parted and there, just above them on the hillside, stood Miles Wilford, his feet planted firmly apart and his hands on his hips.

'Be off with you this instant!' he shouted. 'How dare you harass the Squire's niece. I'll have you flogged for it!'

In an instant they took to their heels, dispersing and vanishing into the trees before their identities could be noted.

Abigail struggled to her feet and stood swaying faintly till Miles stepped forward and took her arm.

'Have they hurt you, Abigail?' he asked solicitously. 'Come, let me take you to shelter.'

'I am not hurt,' she whispered. 'Only shaken. It was a most terrible experience. Thank you for coming to my aid. It was fortunate that you happened to be at hand.' She shuddered. 'Those men—their eyes!'

He slipped an arm round her and began to lead her up the hill to the cottage. 'Try not to think about it, my dear. It is all over now. I warned you that something of this nature might occur. I was afraid of it.'

They entered the cottage and he led her to the settle, lowering her gently on to it. 'It is indeed fortunate, as you say, that I was at hand. I slipped out of church just before the sermon.' He smiled. 'I am afraid Father's sermons are often tedious. I was in no mood for one this morning. I had a fancy to visit this place instead.' He looked around him. 'It is quite cosy, don't you think.' He took a flask from his pocket. 'May I offer you a sip of brandy Abigail? It is most efficacious in cases of shock.'

She shook her head. 'No, I thank you, but it would be wasted on me. I cannot abide the taste—and brandy is too scarce to waste on those who do not appreciate it.'

He took a deep draught himself, laughing as he replaced the flask in his pocket. 'There is no scarcity of it in our house. Father has a cellar full of it.' He sat down beside her and took her hand.

'Are you feeling better now?' There was a low intimate tone in his voice that Abigail was quick to notice and his eyes dropped to her bosom, half exposed where her dress had been torn. 'I am afraid those louts have bruised your lovely flesh, my dear,' he said thickly.

She flushed and looked down at her dishevelled state, trying ineffectively to draw the tattered material together. He put out a hand to stop her, his eyes glittering.

'Please—I find you at your most attractive like this,' he said hoarsely. 'I told you on that other occasion—when I found you riding over the fields so wildly, your hair streaming and your legs bare.' He drew a long shuddering breath. 'You are beautiful, Abigail.' He moved closer to her, but she slipped away from his outstretched hands and rose quickly to her feet, her heart beating fast.

'I—I must go,' she said. 'My uncle is expecting guests and I cannot be seen like this.'

But he moved quickly across the room, slamming the cottage door and standing between her and it. 'Not so fast, Abigail,' he said. 'We have things to say to each other. Why else do you think we are here?'

Her eyes widened as she realized the truth. It had all been a trick. Miles had told the boy to give her the message; had he bribed those

162

louts too and incited them to attack her? She shuddered.

'You have no right to keep me here against my will,' she said. 'Let me go at once or you will pay for it!'

He shook his head at her. 'Is this the way you show your gratitude to me? I could easily say that I found you up here, making yourself free with a gang of village louts!'

Her eyes blazed at him. 'You would never be believed in such a vile lie! You yourself tricked me here. I believe you primed those men with your father's brandy then set them on to me. You gave a bogus message to Toby Bray for me.'

He laughed lazily. 'And you came running, didn't you, Abigail? Because you were expecting to find someone else here!' He stepped up close to her. 'You are well acquainted with this place, are you not? You have been here many times in secret but you did not know that you were observed—that I saw you when you placed the key under the stone with such care. Where do you think I found your locket? It was *here*—in the place where you meet your secret lover. But he shall not have you. You shall be mine first!' He made a lunge at her, grasping her firmly and pressing his thick moist lips to hers.

With a strangled cry she lashed out at his face with her hands, dragging her nails down the flesh of his cheeks till he released her with an angry cry.

'You—you vixen! I believe you *are* a witch! By God, you shall pay for that!' He snatched both her hands and thrust them behind her back, holding them with a strength she would never have suspected his long white hands capable of. She opened her mouth and let out a shrill scream but he laughed sadistically,

'Scream all you like, Abigail. No one comes to Maid's Hill. You yourself have found it the perfect place for an assignation. Now you shall share it with me!' He pushed her back until she could feel the stair rail pressing into her spine, thrusting his face so close to her that she could see the beads of sweat on his brow and the flecks of spittle at the corners of his mouth. 'Refuse me now, Abigail, and the whole county shall know of your secret night visits here with your lover. You will be a social outcast when I have done with you. You would be glad enough then to marry me.'

'How can you speak of marriage?' she asked, twisting in his grasp in an attempt to free herself. 'You behave as though you hate me—you tell people that I practise witchcraft—you say I am wild. Why then do you not leave me alone?'

'I'll *tell* you why!' His voice grated as he pressed himself close to her. 'Because you drive me mad with desire. Because I can think and dream of nothing other than possessing you! Because, damn you, you have *bewitched* me!' He snatched at a handful of her hair, pulling her head back and fastening his lips on hers till she could not breathe nor move.

With every ounce of strength in her body she fought him; kicked, scratched and punched but he seemed oblivious. He was like a madman, charged with superhuman strength as he held her tightly, his hands caressing her roughly. his lips claiming hers again and again till she thought she must suffocate. Weakness began to overtake her as her strength ebbed, but just as she was losing hope there was a sudden rush of air as the door was thrown open and a voice rang out:

'Let her go, damn you!'

The effect on Miles was instant. He released Abigail so abruptly that she staggered back and almost fell. She caught at the stair rail to steady herself and as she did so she swung round to face the owner of the challenging voice, letting out a cry of relief as she saw who it was.

Roget's tall figure filled the doorway, his face dark with anger at the scene that confronted him. For an instant the two men stared at one another then Miles drew in his breath.

'You!' he breathed.

Without taking his eyes from Miles, Roget held out his hand to Abigail. 'My horse is in the copse. Wait for me there.' He took off his coat and put it round her shoulders. 'I shall not be long,' he said grimly. 'I have a matter to attend to.'

Abigail found Roget's horse standing quietly among the trees and stood shivering against his warm flank. Presently she put her arms round the animal's neck and gave way to the tears that rose like a fountain in her. Roget found her like this some moments later. Putting his hands on her shoulders he turned her gently towards him and held her tenderly, stroking her hair.

'All is well now, my darling,' he murmured. 'Come, let me take you home.'

She looked up at him in wonderment. 'How is it that you are here? It was like a miracle, your coming. The answer to my prayer. Oh, Roget—' Tears ran silently down her cheeks and he bent and kissed them away.

'Hush dearest, hush. It will be many a long day before that swine shall come near you again.'

She looked up at him fearfully. 'What what did you do to him? Oh Roget perhaps you should not have crossed him. He has been watching me—he *knows*. I am not sure how much, but certainly that you and I have made night visits to the cottage. He is spiteful and vindictive. He will betray us.'

He smiled grimly. 'I have taught him a lesson this day that he will not forget quickly. He will think twice before he crosses swords with me again.' He kissed her. 'Come now, love, you're trembling. I must take you home.'

'You must not know where I live,' she whispered. 'Take me as far as the cliff path. The sea always calms me.'

He swung her up on to the horse and mounted himself, then he urged the animal down through the trees and on to the road.

They exchanged no words as they rode across the field. He had still not explained to her why he was still in Broomcott. There was so much too that she wanted to tell him, but her head spun with the events of the morning. She still felt faint from her ordeal and she was glad to lean against his hard body, letting her love for him wash over her. It seemed all too soon that they reached the cliff path and he was lifting her down from his horse. He looked down into her eyes.

'I will leave you here. Go and find Bess now, my love. She will take care of you.'

She leaned her weight against him for a moment. 'Oh Roget,' she whispered. 'I have thought so much about the things I said to you yesterday. I was so ashamed, but I confess that I would say it all again.' She looked beseechingly up into his eyes. 'Roget if we truly love each other could we not run away? Could you not take me with you—*now*?'

But he shook his head. 'I can only ask you to trust me, Jenny. Please go home now.' He raised her hands to his lips. 'We shall meet again soon, I promise you.'

167

And all she could do was to watch helplessly as he mounted and rode away along the cliff path.

When Bess saw the condition her mistress was in she threw up her hands in horror.

'Oh my dear Lord, Miss Abi! Whatever've happened to 'ee?' She grasped Abigail's hand and drew her through the kitchen door. 'A good thing Sarah didn't see 'ee lookin' like that Come upstairs and let me see to 'ee. The French gentleman be 'ere and it be close on time for luncheon.'

In her room as she stripped off her torn gown Abigail quickly told Bess of the bogus message she had received, of the frightening confrontation with the witch-hunters and of Miles's contrived 'rescue'. As she listened Bess's mouth gaped in horror.

'Oh, *Miss*! If Mr. Row-jay 'adn't come when 'e did—oh, I daren't think what might've 'appened!' She picked up the tattered gown, looking at it with dismay. 'Your pretty gown be ruined—though maybe I could mend 'un if I tried.'

'You can have it, Bess,' Abigail said with a shudder. 'I could never again wear it without thinking of this morning.' She turned to the girl. 'Oh, Bess, I am so afraid that my uncle may get to hear of all that has happened. If word of any of it reaches his ears he may make me marry Philip Jefferson at once and return to London with him out of the way.'

Bess put an arm round her shoulders. 'Never fear, Miss Abi. The story were put about by them wicked Wilfords an' if I know aught about it that Mr. Miles be a craven coward. He won't dare make no more trouble now that Mr. Row-jay've dealt wi' 'im.' She pursed her lips thoughtfully. 'Though if you takes my advice, Miss, you'll do well to bide a while and let the dust scttle, so to speak.' She fingered the dark bruise on Abigail's shoulder where the stone had hit her. 'Be 'ee well enough to go down, Miss Abi? I could tell the master as you'd a headache and 'ad to lie down.'

Abigail smiled ruefully. 'I doubt if that excuse would meet with much sympathy, Bess. No, if Monsieur Dupont is here I shall be expected to play hostess. Fetch my blue gown and some hot water to wash the dirt from my face and hands.'

When Bess returned from the kitchen with the can of water her face was red and she was out of breath.

'Make haste, Miss, do! The master says you're to come down directly. Mr. Philip've arrived and they're all a'waitin' for you in the drawin'-room.'

Abigail felt as though her heart had almost stopped beating as she hurriedly washed and pulled on her gown. Bess took a brush and tugged at the thick, tangled hair.

'Oh, hold still, *do*, Miss Abi,' she
169

commanded. 'Your 'air be so thick'n curly it be 'orse's work to make 'un lie tidy! There now—' She tucked the last tendril into place and took a step back to survey her mistress's appearance. 'No one'd ever guess that ten minutes since you looked as if you'd been dragged at the cart's tail!'

Abigail sighed. 'I feel as though I have that experience in store, Bess!' She stood in the middle of the room twisting her hands together nervously, suddenly sorely afraid. 'Oh, Bess,' she cried. 'What is to become of me?'

The girl took both her mistress's hands in her own red, work-roughened ones. 'There be only one thing 'ee can do, Miss,' she said gently. 'Take each piece o' the cake as it comes. It be only when you'm chewed one piece that you can bite off another.'

The little piece of homespun logic worked wonders for Abigail—it made her smile. Bess was quite right, she reflected. One could take but one problem at a time and that was what she would do—the most immediate being to get her initial meeting with Philip Jefferson over with. She took a deep breath and straightened her shoulders.

'Very well—I am ready. Will you walk down with me, Bess?'

Bess smiled and patted her arm lightly. 'That's the spirit. That be my Miss Abi!'

They parted company in the hall outside the

drawingroom door and Abigail gathered together all her courage while Bess mouthed her encouragement and flapped her hands towards the door.

Just inside the room stood her uncle in earnest conversation with a small, swarthy man dressed in black. They turned as she came in and her uncle performed the grimace that for him passed as a smile.

'Ah, Abigail, my dear. Allow me to present Monsieur Claude Dupont, of whom you have heard me speak. My niece, Abigail Labeque.'

The little Frenchman took her hand and raised it to his lips in a courtly salute, his quick brown eyes darting over her.

'*Enchanté*, Mademoiselle,' he said gravely.

Abigail dropped a curtsey, '*Merci, Monsieur. J'espère que vous passerez une visite aimable.*'

Thomas cleared his throat impatiently. 'Abigail—our other guest is waiting to be presented to you.' He held out his hand. 'My stepson, Philip.'

Following the direction of his hand as he stood aside, Abigail noticed for the first time the tall broad figure standing in the window alcove. He turned now and came towards her with a smile. His clothes were expertly cut and of the latest fashion, his boots of the finest leather and his waistcoat boasting the new wide lapels worn outside his coat. But these details went unnoticed by Abigail. She was

171

staring incredulously at his face—a face that was both known and loved by her—the face of her beloved 'Roget'.

CHAPTER TEN

How she kept herself from crying out, she would never know. Philip Jefferson crossed the room quickly and raised her hand to his lips, but as he did so, his eyes caught hers. In them the message was as clear as though he had spoken and, taking a deep breath, she managed to control the turmoil within her.

'I am glad to make your acquaintance at last, sir,' she said, her voice trembling a little.

He smiled. 'I too, Mademoiselle—though surely it is unneccesary for us to be so formal, especially as we are to be betrothed. I hope—indeed *insist*—that you call me Philip, whilst I myself confess that I yearn to use your delightful Christian name—Abigail.'

She was taken aback. He spoke like an entirely different person, his tone and inflection affected and exaggerated and his mode of dress—the pomaded hair and the whiff of perfume as he bent over her hand—they were all so alien to her 'Roget'. Was it possible that she had been mistaken after all? But the next moment she was reassured. Her uncle and Monsieur Dupont had moved to the

172

other end of the room, their heads bent in earnest conversation. Philip pressed her hand lightly and lowered his voice.

'Trust me, dearest. I will explain everything to you at the first opportunity.'

She drew in her breath sharply as she remembered something. Bess! If she were to be suddenly confronted by 'Roget' when she came in to serve the meal she might well give all of them away! Returning the pressure of Philip's hand she turned to her uncle and Monsieur Dupont.

'If you will excuse me I must make sure that all is well in the kitchen,' she said and slipped out into the hall.

Thomas Hargreaves beamed at his stepson. 'Well, what did I tell you? Is she not a handsome young woman? She is efficient in the running of household matters too—good with the servants and as well educated as is good for a woman to be. Have I not chosen well for you?'

Philip smiled lazily. 'I daresay she will prove an amusing enough diversion during my short, infrequent stays at Broomcott,' he drawled with a glance towards the door. 'Indeed, I may even take to coming to the Manor more often in future.'

Thomas frowned. 'You will marry the girl though. I'll have no dallying! Besides, the Manor needs a lady in residence again.'

Philip shrugged and smothered a yawn, 'As

you wish, sir. Now I must go and see if that fellow Harker has attended to my horse adequately. I'll see you anon.'

Abigail found Bess in the passage that led from the kitchen to the buttery and breathlessly spilled out her incredible news. Bess's eyes grew round as saucers.

'You mean—you mean as you'm been betrothed to Mr. *Row-jay* all the time an' didn't know it?' she gasped.

'Yes!' Joyful laughter bubbled in Abigail's voice. 'Oh, Bess, I can hardly believe it yet there is still so much that I do not understand. My head is spinning with it all! I knew I must warn you though, before you came in to serve dinner and saw for yourself.'

'Oh!' Bess's hand flew to her mouth. 'Oh—I'm that glad you did, Miss Abi. I'd 'a dropped the dinner fer sure—an' that would never'a' done, would it?' She threw her arms impulsively round her mistress. 'Oh, Miss Abi, I'm fair pleased fer'ee. As 'appy as if t'were me and Jack.'

Abigail hugged her. 'Thank you, Bess dear. Now I must go or they will wonder what has become of me.'

Over the meal Abigail listened in wonder to Philip Jefferson's conversation. His talk of life in the Beaumonde, and the fashionable round of theatres, balls and entertainments. Her heart grew heavy as she listened to his drawling, affected tones. Could this really be

174

the man she had fallen so deeply in love with? He sounded more like the creature she had heard described by the servants and the Wilfords, the Philip Jefferson she had come to despise: a pleasure-loving parasite, interested only in himself. How *could* he and Roget be the same man? Perhaps in spite of what he had said, there had been a mistake.

Claude Dupont spoke hardly at all during the meal but Abigail saw a look pass between him and her uncle as they were finishing their dessert. Thomas Hargreaves looked up, clearing his throat and cut in just as Philip was recounting an anecdote about the gaming club to which he belonged.

'As Monsieur Dupont and I have business to discuss I will excuse you from taking port with us, Philip. No doubt you and Abigail will have matters to talk over. It is a pleasant evening. I am sure she would enjoy showing you the garden she has made. We will join you later.'

Philip looked across the table at Abigail. 'I would be enchanted to see the garden.' He stood up and offered her his arm. 'Will you be so kind?'

They walked out of the house in silence but as soon as they had turned the corner and passed out of sight through the gate in the wall his arms were around her, his lips seeking hers hungrily. Abigail's heart quickened.

'Oh, Roget, it is like a miracle—a dream come true,' she whispered.

He kissed her tenderly. 'You must not call me 'Roget' now, my love. Oh, there is so much to explain to you. May we go somewhere where we shall not be overheard?'

'The garden is as good a place as any— come.' She took his hand and led him to the opening in the tall yew hedge but when he saw the garden spread before him, Philip drew in his breath sharply.

'Why—it is just as I remember it as a child!' He turned to look at her. 'My mother loved this garden. When I was very small, in the days before I went away to school—when my own father was alive, she would bring me out here with her to play hide and seek in the shrubbery.' He sighed. 'How very long ago it seems. But you have re-created it, Abigail, just as you re-created my life when you came into it.' He smiled down at her then his smile faded as he saw her bewildered expression. 'Oh, my poor darling. You must have been wondering what manner of man it was that you had pledged your love to. There is so much to tell you, I hardly know where to begin.'

They had reached the arbour and she led him into the soft, rose-scented dimness. He looked down at her for a moment, taking both of her hands in his, then he drew her close, encircling her in his arms and kissing her long and deeply.

'Oh, Abigail, if you could only know what it means to me, coming here and finding that

176

you are the girl I have loved all along.' He pressed his lips against her hair.

She looked up at him. 'But knowing the village and the people who live here as you do, did you not guess?'

He smiled. 'I did, but a guess was all it was and I had to be sure, I would not have dared to declare myself to you until I was. If my Jenny had not been Abigail Labeque after all I would have revealed my identity needlessly. I would not have risked putting so great a burden on the girl I loved. That was why I asked you to wait to trust me. It pained me to see you go away so upset and when I received your sweet little note it was all I could do to stop myself rushing straight to you at once.' He kissed her again. 'But now all is well—*wonderfully* well!'

Abigail looked up at him, biting her lip. 'One thing puzzles me: the way you spoke at dinner—and the way I have heard people describe you—it is all so *unlike* you. I mean so unlike Roget the man I love.'

He sat down on the little bench and drew her down beside him. 'Oh, my love, you are so confused and little wonder. There is so much you do not know about me and I must try to explain it all to you. When my mother married Thomas Hargreaves, your uncle, I was still at school and it was only when I came home that I realized my father had died without leaving a will. The entire estate had passed to my mother, my being under age, and when she

177

remarried my stepfather gained control—though she had managed to persuade him to put some money in trust for me. After Mother died life became intolerable. My stepfather allowed me no say in how the estate was run and eventually I went to live in London with friends. For a short while I lived the kind of life you heard me describe tonight, but I soon grew tired of it. I wanted to be of use in the world—to live like a man. Then I heard of this plan to smuggle French refugee children across the channel to safety in England. I begged to take part in it and I have never regretted being given the opportunity.'

Abigail nodded. 'I see—but why do you let people go on thinking you are thoughtless and pleasure-seeking?'

He smiled. 'It suits me very well. No one troubles to lower their voice in the presence of a simple-minded fop. I have learned a lot through keeping my affected character.' He laughed gently, his eyes teasing her. 'Did you think that was my true nature after all, sweetheart? I must be a better actor than I thought!'

She joined in his laughter, greatly relieved. 'But you did not return to London yesterday after all?'

His eyes grew serious and he gripped her hands. 'I have been worried lately about the suffering caused by my stepfather's plans for enclosing the Manor lands. You may not know

178

that before he married my mother he owned a textile mill in Lancashire. It was failing and I thought he had sold it, but I have lately discovered that it is flourishing. He has enlarged it and installed new machinery. This is obviously why he intends to turn most of our land over to sheep—to provide his own raw material.' He looked at her. 'All this—and the fact that I wanted to meet my betrothed—made it imperative that I visit Broomcott at the earliest possible opportunity and I have found one thing at least to tell me I was right to come.'

He kissed her gently and she laid her head on his shoulder happily for a moment. Then she remembered something.

'Philip—' She looked up at him, her eyes troubled. 'It may not be safe in future to land the children in the cove. I am so afraid of what Miles Wilford might do.'

He gave a light laugh. 'He will do nothing—not after the lesson I taught him this afternoon. He is no different now than he was as a boy. There has never been any love lost between us but he was never in any doubt as to who would come off worst in a quarrel. He is the biggest coward I know!'

But Abigail gripped his arm. 'You do not know everything though. Miles has formed a wish to marry me. When I first spurned him he tried to spread the word that I was a witch. Today he incited a gang of youths to intimidate me and then pretended to rescue me from them. He tricked me into being alone with him at the cottage and he told me that he had seen me meeting someone there. I have no idea whether he knows it was you. He threatened to besmirch my name unless I—' She lowered her eyes, trembling at the memory of the afternoon's horror and Philip drew her close.

'I only thank God that I heard your screams. I was on my way to the Manor. I had been to the inn at Dorchester to change my clothes.' He looked down at her, his eyes dark. 'It was all I could do to control myself. I wanted to wring his scrawny neck.'

She shook her head. 'But don't you see, dearest, if he knows of your secret work with the children he has a sound way of getting his revenge. He need not raise a finger to you himself.'

Philip pressed her hand warmly. 'There is no need to worry, my love. Operations have been halted, for the time being, anyway. For some time now, Paul and I have had our suspicions about the safety of the children and their well-being after they have left our custody. That was why Paul himself undertook the care of the last and youngest of them. Some time ago our associate in France was caught and executed. Someone else took his place but we have grave doubts about his loyalty. We have reason to believe that the

180

money and valuables may be finding their way into the wrong hands and that the children may again be in danger. Paul has been making investigations and I am to ride into Dorchester on Tuesday to confer with him.' He drew her close and his eyes grew tender. 'And now, dearest, let us not talk any more of sadness and fear.' He shook his head. 'Being here with you like this is still like a dream to me and I still cannot quite believe that I shall not wake in a moment and find you gone.'

For a while they were silent, content to be together, lost in the joy of their love for each other. Then Philip lifted his head as the sound of voices drifted across the garden on the still evening air.

'It is my stepfather and his friend. They said they would join us.' He looked at her. 'By the way, who *is* Monsieur Dupont? Why is he here, do you know?'

'All I know is that he has come here to discuss business,' Abigail told him.

He frowned. 'I do not see what a man like that would have to do with the enclosure of English land-still less with a textile mill. Perhaps he is a money lender.'

As they stepped out of the arbour together Thomas Hargreaves and his companion were coming towards them across the grass. Dusk was falling now and the shadows were lengthening. Philip pressed her hand and called out to his stepfather, re-assuming the affected, flippant tones he had used before:

'Ah—there you are, Father. What a delightful garden Abigail has made and what an enchanting companion she is, to be sure.'

Thomas beamed at them both. 'You are well suited. I knew it and I am always right in these matters. I hope you have decided on a date for the wedding. I see no reason to wait.'

Philip nodded. 'I propose to ask Abigail to accompany me to London. I am anxious to show her off to my friends. I think it might be as well if the wedding were to take place there too, as it is where all my friends are.'

Thomas frowned. 'It would be most irregular for the future squire to be married away from his own parish. A wedding creates goodwill and that is something we are in need of in Broomcott at present.'

As stepfather and son moved away, Abigail glanced at the little Frenchman. He was silent but she saw that his eyes missed nothing. They darted about like black fireflies and when they lighted upon her she felt uneasy. She walked towards him, forcing herself to smile.

'Monsieur, I know that you have lived in England now for a long time, but if it would please you to speak in your own language I should be delighted to have conversation with you.'

The man's lips stretched themselves into a smile but his eyes remained the same: alert and wary. 'You are very kind, Mademoiselle, but I prefer to speak in English. I am as comfortable with it now as with my mother-tongue.'

Abigail nodded. 'As you wish, sir.'

When they reached the drawing-room Philip and Thomas were still arguing about where the wedding should take place and Abigail stepped between them.

'If I might be allowed an opinion,' she ventured. 'I should like best of all to be married at St. Dominic's, but as I know this cannot be I would like to be married here at St. Catherine's. As Uncle Thomas says, a wedding creates goodwill and I have many friends among the people of the village.' She moved to Philip's side and placed her fingers lightly on his arm. 'Afterwards, if it were possible, I would like to go to Salisbury to have my marriage blessed by Father Jeremy. Would you allow me to have my way in this one small thing, sir?'

Philip smiled. 'How can I refuse when you ask so prettily. But we will compromise—you shall come with me to London first. You will need to buy your trousseau at least.'

Abigail looked at Thomas, her eyes shining. 'May I, Uncle? I could take Bess with me as chaperon.'

Thomas Hargreaves looked positively benign as he beamed at them. 'Well, I see no objection—as long as you see that Wilford fellow first about putting up the banns. Better do it first thing tomorrow.'

He left them and went to Claude Dupont, taking him by the arm and moving towards the door and out of the room. Abigail looked at Philip.

'First thing tomorrow! I do not relish the thought of visiting the Wilford household,' she said, biting her lip.

He shook his head. 'It will be well to get it over and done with. I must also go to the place where I hid the child's belongings on the night of the raid. I must take them to Paul when I go. I only hope that they are safe.'

Abigail drew in her breath. 'Dearest, your arm! I forgot to ask you—how is the wound?'

Gently, he caught her hand, preventing it from touching his arm and, with a glance in the direction of the open door, he said quietly: 'It is well now, healing fast, but I must keep it concealed. By now everyone in the village will know that there was a raid and that at least one excise bullet found its mark. All eyes will be alert for injuries.'

She nodded. 'Of course—but are you sure it is healing? Can I not dress it for you?'

He smiled and touched her cheek. 'I promise you it is well, love. I am keeping it clean and covered. Soon there will be no trace of it, I assure you, though I love you for your sweet concern.' He raised her chin with one finger. 'But now, sweetheart I think you should retire. We have much to do tomorrow and you

184

have lost a great deal of sleep lately—all on my account.'

His look of tenderness made her heart contract. It was so long since there had been anyone to care for her like this. She wanted to reach up and kiss him, to feel him close to her, his heart beating against her own. Instead she touched his cheek softly with her finger-tip.

'Goodnight then, dearest,' she said. 'I will see you in the morning. Will you dream of me?' she added in a whisper.

He bent and brushed her lips with his. 'I can dream of nothing else, darling,' he said, his lips against her cheek.

*   *   *

Miles and Rebecca Wilford were in the morning-room at the Parsonage. It was now more than twenty-four hours since Miles had received a thrashing at the hands of Philip Jefferson and now the bruise around his left eye was purple and black, the lid puffy and the eyeball angrily bloodshot. Rebecca was making a clumsy attempt at holding a dripping piece of beefsteak to it and muttering furiously to herself as she did so.

'Of all the stupidity! Surely you did not really believe that you could win the wretched girl's affections by such clumsy methods? And then—allowing yourself to be *thrashed*! What a

185

humiliation! And you call yourself a man!'

Miles glowered up at her from under the steak. 'You need not feel humiliated, sister. It is hardly likely that Philip Jefferson will call on *you* now that he is betrothed to Abigail Labeque.'

She smiled pityingly. 'How can you be so feeble-minded. You have only to tell him of her secret assignations, you fool. He will drop her like a hot brick when he knows the kind of woman she is. When we have finished with her she will be glad enough to marry even *you*.' She smirked to herself. 'Then we shall see who comes off best. When she comes to live at the Parsonage—with you for a husband and me for a sister-in-law—then we shall see some sport, brother!'

He glanced up at her. 'I have my own ideas about that lover of hers. I believe he is in some way connected with smuggling. The man who joins her when she goes to the cottage is always carrying something that looks heavy. I wonder if he was wounded in the raid the other night?'

Rebecca frowned. 'But you said she did not go to the cottage that night.'

He shook his head. 'She may have done for all I know. When I heard the shots I did not stay to see.'

His sister snorted. 'You didn't go to the beach to find out what was happening either, did you? You scuttled home like a frightened rabbit! You really are a dolt, brother. That was the one night that you might have learned the truth about the lovely Abigail!'

He glared at her. 'It is very easy for you to talk. You have not spent night after night getting soaked to the skin as I have, watching-most of the time in vain.'

But Rebecca hardly heard him, she was deep in speculation, her eyes half closed. 'I must ask around the village and keep my eyes open for an injured man,' she mused. 'No dead body was found—nor yet a badly wounded man, so who ever it was must have sustained a flesh wound—and our little Abigail is skilled in the attention of such things, is she not?' She spoke half to herself as she paced the room, but she came to a halt by the window as the sound of horses on the drive outside brought her attention back to the present.

'Speak of the Devil!' she exclaimed, looking out of the window. 'Here is Abigail now, riding up to the front door as large as life—and with Philip Jefferson too!' She peered out. 'I must say she seems mighty amiable with him for one whose affections lie elsewhere.' She watched as they dismounted and handed their reins to the Parsonage groom. 'Mmm—' She bit at her thumb nail thoughtfully. 'I declare, Philip Jefferson handles his mount gingerly for a country-bred man. I would have almost thought—' She turned to her brother. 'No doubt they have come to enquire after your *health!'*

Miles rose to his feet with such haste that the slab of beefsteak fell with a plop on to the carpet. 'I—I do not wish to see them,' he stammered. 'Tell them—tell them I am out!' and he rushed from the room in confusion, leaving his sister rocking with mirth. As the door closed behind him she stopped laughing, her eyes narrowing as a thought struck her. Yes—the puzzle was beginning to fall into place!

Parson Wilford was somewhat taken aback to see Abigail and Philip, although he had already learned of their betrothal from his irate daughter. That conniving fellow, Hargreaves, must have known all along that neither his niece or his stepson were free and yet he had done all he could to encourage the hopes of his own dear Miles and Rebecca. He was mightily glad now that he had refused to preach the sermon the fellow would have had him preach. What did Hargreaves think he was—a tool, to be manipulated to his advantage? Oh no, he had his own axe to grind—and it had nothing to do with sheep!

When the maidservant showed Philip and Abigail into his study, however, he was a picture of rosy benevolence. He asked politely after Thomas's health and spoke welcomingly to Philip. The wedding date was arranged for one month ahead and all the necessary particulars noted. He was just about to show them out when the door opened and Rebecca entered. She had hurriedly changed into a gown of rich gold taffeta which, although too elaborate for the morning, suited her better than anything else Abigail had seen her wear. She carried a heavy lace fan with ribs of ivory which she fluttered coyly, smiling over it at Philip as she spoke to her father:

'Papa, I am ashamed of you. The girl has only just told me that we have visitors and here you are letting them go without offering them refreshments.'

'We are not here on a social call,' Philip said quickly. 'We have come to ask your father to put up the banns for our marriage before Abigail and I leave for London in a few days' time.'

Rebecca's face took on a waxy sheen, but the smile remained firmly fixed to her face. 'I have heard of your betrothal from your charming fiancée, Mr Jefferson. But I must confess that I think you are a very bad man not to have told me of it when we met in London recently. Why, I declare, you flirted with me quite outrageously!' She lifted the heavy fan and flicked his left arm with it. Caught unawares, Philip winced and drew in his breath sharply. Rebecca instantly perceived this, her small green eyes narrowing and glinting triumphantly.

'Oh! Did I hurt you? I am so sorry, but I would not have thought it possible—' She gazed at the fan in her hand with a bewildered expression and Abigail spoke quickly:

'Philip's horse threw him yesterday,' she said. 'His shoulder and arm are still tender and bruised.'

Rebecca shook her head. 'Do forgive me. My brother also is suffering from bruising. I know how painful it is. I am so clumsy!'

When they were out of sight of the house Philip reined his mount to a halt, catching Bobby's bridle to halt him too. Abigail looked at him in surprise.

'What is it?'

He drew his left arm across his chest and she gave a gasp of alarm as she noticed the dark stain on his sleeve.

'Oh! Your wound—it is bleeding again. Does it pain you?'

He shook his head, his expression grim. 'It is nothing compared to the nagging uncertainty I feel. Was that playful tap an accident or a calculated test? And was the blood on my sleeve visible before we left the parsonage?'

*   *   *

Rebecca paced the floor of her bedroom restlessly, pausing from time to time to gaze out of the window. Where had that good-for-nothing brother of hers got to? They must have certain proof of Philip Jefferson's guilt and have it soon! Rebecca seethed with jealous

190

fury. She had learned this evening from the kitchen girl, who was distantly related to Sarah, the Manor cook, that Philip was taking Abigail to London to buy her trousseau and to introduce her into the Beau-monde. *Abigail!* It wasn't fair! The wretched girl had nothing except her face and figure—it was said that she even had no dowry—and yet Philip Jefferson was obviously besotted with her! She stamped her foot, her cheeks crimson with frustration as angry tears coursed down them. If only they could find some shred of evidence. She had all but proved that Philip had some injury to his arm as she had suspected. If only she herself could have gone to the Dolphin tonight. Miles was such a weakling. She was sure she could have done better than him—the dunderhead.

Half an hour later the little French clock on the mantel struck one and her frustrated patience was rewarded as the door opened and Miles came in. He was breathless and his clothes were dishevelled and dirty. She crossed the room quickly and grasped him by the lapels of his coat.

'Well, brother—what news?'

He thrust her from him impatiently. 'For God's sake allow me to catch my breath, woman!' He flopped into a chair. 'I need something to drink and a rest.'

Rebecca snorted derisively and poured him a glass of water from the carafe on her night table, pushing the glass under his nose with a

191

look of scorn.

'Here, weakling—drink it before you are taken with the vapours!'

He drank the water at a single draught, ignoring her cutting remarks. Then he looked up, his eyes glinting. 'The Dolphin was all but empty,' he said. 'It made me suspicious, so I went to the cliffs and found a place to hide where I could watch the cove. I had to wait a long time, but it was worth it. I *saw* them, Rebecca—men landing a cargo of some sort. Contraband for sure. They beached the boat and used a path close to where I was hiding. I saw them carrying it—kegs, boxes—a good haul by the look of it. And that's not all?' He learned forward, his pale face flushed. 'I heard them talking and their next job is two weeks from tonight. We have them, Rebecca! Just think of it.

She chewed her lip. 'Yes, but was *he* with them? Did you see him?'

He shook his head. 'Not then—but later, just as I was about to leave my hiding place, I heard a noise. I looked out and saw him.'

Her eyes sparkled. 'What was he doing?'

'I couldn't tell at first. He seemed to be scrabbling at the rock. Then I saw him lift out a box—a heavy box. You see what this means, don't you, Rebecca? He is one of them! I was right.'

She glared at him. 'I was right, you mean! It was I who discovered he had been wounded.'

Her eyes narrowed. 'But two weeks from tonight, you say? Surely the two love-birds will be in London then?'

Miles smiled triumphantly. 'Really, sister! And you consider yourself so clever! Do you not see—it is a ruse!'

'You—you mean it is merely a tale they are putting about to make people think they are far away—when all the time they will be here?' She clapped her hands in delight. 'You are right, brother. We *have* them! A month from now they will not stand at the altar, but in the dock where they belong!'

CHAPTER ELEVEN

Abigail sat alone in the rose arbour, thinking of Philip. He had left Broomcott for Dorchester at first light and already she was missing him. When they had returned from the Parsonage yesterday she had dressed the reopened wound, relieved to find only a small break in the newly healed skin. Fortunately, there had been no one at home and so she and Bess had attended to it in Abigail's room. Afterwards she and Philip had come down here to the garden to talk. Sitting here in the arbour she had explained to him how the money her father had left for her in an English bank had dwindled away.

'I have no dowry to bring you,' she said sadly. 'It makes me unhappy to think that I come to you in such poverty. I know it would have grieved my poor Papa too.'

He had kissed her. 'What does money matter, love? All I shall ever want is here in my arms at this moment.'

But Abigail frowned, troubled as she had often been at the unanswered question in her mind concerning the money.

'Philip—'she looked up at him. 'Why do you suppose the Sisters needed my money? As soon as Papa could send no more to pay for my education I began working for them instead. I always understood this was sufficient to earn my keep.'

He looked puzzled. 'I do not understand. The Sisters could not touch your money. What gave you the idea that they could?'

'Uncle Thomas,' she said at once. 'He said that the money was gone long ago and that I was dependent on his charity—his good nature.'

Philip laughed dryly. 'Good nature! That is rich indeed. But there is something very wrong here. No one could have had access to the bank account except your legally appointed guardian. He stopped in mid-sentence and looked at her. 'Have you the name of the bank?'

She nodded. 'I still have the letter that was deposited with the bank and sent to me at the convent on poor Papa's death.

He turned to her, urgency in his eyes. 'Will you fetch it, Abigail? Will you let me see it?'

She had fetched it and he had read it carefully, his face grave. Finally he had said: 'May I keep this for the time being, Abigail? While I am away I will go to Winchester and make enquiries.'

She looked at him, her face eager. 'You think the money may still be there after all?'

He shook his head. 'I fear not, my love. What I am afraid of is that you may have been cheated out of this money and I mean to find out by whom.'

This morning she had risen early to breakfast with him before he left and he had told her quietly that he had slipped out during the night to recover the valuables he had hidden on the night of the raid. He showed her the stout box as he packed it with the rest of his belongings for the journey.

'Paul will be glad to have it,' he told her. 'I know that he intends to invest it for the child's future. I was greatly relieved to find it intact and safe.'

Before he had mounted he had pulled her into his arms and kissed her, then instructed Bess, who stood close by, to take good care of her mistress in his absence. As he rode out through the gates Bess sighed wistfully.

'Oh, Miss Abi—'e be *so* 'andsome. I reckon your troubles be over now. Soon you'll be a 'livin' 'appy ever after—like in the fairy tales.'

Abigail shook her head. 'Something tells me we still have some difficulties to overcome, Bess,' she said and went slowly back into the house, Bess following with a bewildered expression on her homely face.

The leaves rustled in the breeze that had sprung up and Abigail shivered slightly. It had turned chilly, she had not noticed the evening falling, so preoccupied had she been with her own thoughts. Where was Philip now, she wondered. No doubt he was with Paul. Although she knew he faced no danger on this occasion she would not know a moment's peace until he was with her again.

She stood up. It must be almost time for dinner. Her uncle had been out all day with Monsieur Dupont, showing him round the village and the estate. They would surely be back soon, hungry for their evening meal. She had better see how the preparations for it were progressing. But she had only just stepped out of the arbour when she saw Bess coming through the gateway. When she saw Abigail she looked relieved.

'Oh, Miss Abi, there you be. Your uncle wants to see 'ee in 'is study. You'm to make 'aste 'cos 'e baint changed for dinner yet.'

Abigail's eyebrows lifted. Changing for dinner was a new departure for her uncle. He never bothered when they were alone. And what could he want with her? She hoped it

196

would not take too long, also that she had not incurred his displeasure. She was not in the mood for one of his lectures.

She tapped on the heavy oak door and entered to find him as usual, resting his goutly leg on a stool while his dog lay close by his side. As she came in he lifted the corners of his mouth amiably.

'Ah, Abigail. Shut the door and come and sit down. I wish to speak to you.'

Quietly, she did as he said, wondering what it was he could have to say. It was clear that he was not displeased at least. When she was seated he nodded at her, his small eyes thoughtful and his lips pursed. He brought the tips of his fingers together and looked at her over the tops of them.

'I wish to tell you that I am well pleased with you, niece,' he said. 'I know that you were opposed to betrothal with my stepson, Philip, and yet you have seen sense and become suitably submissive; something, I confess, I never thought to see in you. It must be that my influence has been brought to bear as it should and I am glad. We shall have a lady at Broomcott, Philip shall have a wife to steady him and you shall have a good life—and all without a dowry, for which you should be—and I am sure you *are*—grateful.' He shifted his position, stretching his leg and grunting slightly. Abigail cleared her throat.

'Is there anything I can do for you, Uncle?'

she asked.

He nodded. 'Indeed there is, child. Although Philip has known you only a short time, I can see that he is taken with you. I want you to try to persuade him to make his home here at Broomcott. To leave London and take up the running of the estate. For some time I have thought to retire and return to my native Lancashire. It may not be easy, but will you try to use your powers of persuasion with him?'

She nodded eagerly, knowing that it would be just what Philip would like. But what could have happened to change her uncle so? The next moment he surprised her even further: reaching into his waistcoat pocket he brought out a small package wrapped in silk.

'Here, child, a small betrothal present for you.' He thrust it into her hands.

Astonished, Abigail unwrapped the gift and found that it was a little patch-box, made in silver, the top enamelled with an exquisite pattern of flowers in pastel colours. When she pressed the catch the lid sprang open, playing a sweet, tinkling tune. She looked up, her eyes shining.

'Oh, Uncle, how pretty! And how kind of you. Thank you so much.' She rose and bent to kiss his cheek but he raised his arm as though to fend off a blow.

'Enough—enough—only a token—a gee-gaw. Away with you now, girl, or we shall both be late for dinner!'

Alone in her room, Abigail sat looking at the patch-box, turning it over in her hands and admiring the workmanship. It really was exquisite. She saw from the underside that it had been made in France and bore the signature of the craftsman. She would never have credited her uncle with such fine taste and she wondered if Monsieur Dupont could have had anything to do with the choice. Smiling, she put it away and began to dress for dinner.

The meal was a silent affair. Without Philip the conversation flagged. Thomas Hargreaves seemed ill at ease for some reason and after the dessert, Abigail was glad to make an excuse and go to her room, but once there she found that the thought of going to bed was unwelcome. Although she had risen early she did not feel sleepy and for a while she sat at the window, watching the stars and thinking of Philip. Finally, too restless for inactivity, she decided to take a walk in the garden.

Her feet made no noise as she slipped down the stairs in her soft kid slippers. It was late, a little after midnight, and she knew that Bess and Sarah had retired long ago. The house was in darkness save for the moonlight that slanted in through the windows, bathing everything in a cool, silver light. Halfway across the hall she stopped. There were voices coming from her uncle's study. Quiet voices, it was true, but in the silence she could hear them quite clearly—

her uncle's and Monsieur Dupont's. So the little Frenchman was capable of conversation after all!

She crept closer to the door and listened. Her uncle had usually retired long before this. What could be keeping him up so late? But Thomas's voice was raised and harsh and it was soon obvious that the two men were engaged in some kind of argument.

'Surely you cannot really believe that I am getting free labour, man?' Thomas thundered. 'The creatures have to be fed and clothed—housed too. All this costs money. There is plenty of cheap labour about, God knows. I am getting nothing out of it at all!'

'Then what do you propose?' the Frenchman asked.

There was a thump as Thomas's fist struck the table. 'Propose? Why, my share of the proceeds, of course! My *fair* share!'

'Impossible, *mon ami*. France needs all the money available. Soon there will be war—war with other countries—perhaps even England herself. Your job is to take the children. They could be disposed of easily enough it is true, but I am a humane man. I make you a gift of them in exchange for the small amount of organization you do for us.'

Thomas growled. 'Gift! Liability, you mean! While there are Englishmen working on this scheme you cannot dispose of the children and you know it. You would be found out and your little money-making scheme would be spoilt. All you had to do was to make sure that the man at the end of the chain was *your* man. You secured me by making certain promises to me. Have you now conveniently forgotten them?'

There was a small silence, then the Frenchman said:

'I promised to make it worth your while, nothing more.'

'But it isn't you *haven't*!' Again his fist came down hard on the table. 'You foreigners are all the same. You make promises you have no intention of keeping—anything to achieve your own ends.'

'But I tell you, my friend—our glorious revolution is costing money,' Dupont insisted. 'Danton must be routed—there is still much to do. Victims are a necessary part of any cause. This, I personally regret, but—'

'*Poppycock!*' Thomas spluttered, almost beside himself with rage. 'If you think I am going to be one of the victims of your revolution, you are very much mistaken. I entered this to make money—as I believe you did. I have put in a lot of work, maintaining all the secrecy you required was not easy—and all for what? For *nothing*! I have been *tricked*! If you want to know, my fine friend, I *hate* your revolution and all it stands for! Who wants to be ruled by a stinking mob anyway, dammit? Thank God I am a civilized Englishman!'

There was a scraping noise as the

Frenchman rose to his feet, his anger aroused at last. 'You will be sorry,' he said in a dangerously low voice. 'Soon the people here in England will rise, you will see. The way that you use them here in Broomcott will ascertain it! You steal their land—you starve them out. I hope that yours will be one of the first heads to roll in the dust. I bid you goodnight!'

Abigail darted back into the shadows just in time as the study door was wrenched open and the stiff, upright figure in black strode angrily out and up the stairs, his feet making staccato cracks like gunfire on every tread. As she pressed herself against the wall she heard her uncle muttering to himself furiously and the clink of glass on glass as he poured himself a generous measure of brandy.

Swift and silent as a shadow she ran lightly back up the stairs to her own room and, closing the door softly behind her, she leaned against it, her heart hammering in her breast.

God in Heaven, so that was it! Monsieur Dupont was the 'Eagle', or rather the man who had replaced him. All this time she had been a member of a group organized by her own uncle for his own avaricious gain! Philip had been right there *was* a great deal wrong. Oh, if only he were here now. He would know what to do. Somehow those poor trusting children must be found and freed from their abominable slavery. And to think that she and Philip had unwittingly delivered them into it!

She waited on the Dorchester road, standing by the patient Bobby as he cropped the grass at the foot of Maid's Hill. From time to time she glanced towards the bend in the road, her ears strained for the sound of a horse. It was the third day she had waited like this. Philip had been gone four days and yet he had said he would be back by the second. Her heart was heavy. What could have happened? Every day that slipped by was precious. Already Monsieur Dupont had departed. He must have left early on the morning after the quarrel. He had not been at breakfast next morning and Thomas had muttered something about his having an urgent appointment.

She sighed despondently and began to lead Bobby back towards the Manor. Another day and she must return without him. Then she stopped—her head on one side as her ears caught the distant sound of hoof-beats. Could it be? She hardly dared hope. She turned, shading her eyes against the brilliance of the setting sun and waited for the horseman to round the bend.

At last her patience was rewarded. A dark-coloured horse emerged, bearing a male rider, his cloak flying as he bent low over the animal's head. Her heart lifted as she raised her hand in greeting.

'Philip!' she cried.

He reined his mount to a halt beside her. 'Abigail! What brings you here? Is all well?'

She ran forward to grasp the bridle. 'No— no, it is not. Come to the cottage. I must talk to you.'

Once within the shelter of the cottage they went into each other's arms. For the moment all was forgotten except their need of each other. Philip kissed her deeply.

'Oh, it is so good to be back with you again, my love,' he whispered. 'I have missed you so and I have much to tell you, but first, let me look at you. It is strange, but when we are apart I cannot recall your sweet face.'

Looking up into his eyes all the anxieties of the past few days seemed to dissolve. Philip was here with her again. Nothing could go too badly wrong, surely, as long as they were together. She stood on tiptoe to take his face between her hands and gently kiss his lips.

'Oh, my dearest,' she breathed. 'I am only half a being when we are apart. Now I am whole again.'

Together they sat down on the settle, their fingers entwined and Abigail looked up anxiously at his face.

'You look weary. Have you ridden far today?'

He nodded. 'All the way from Winchester. I was determined to be with my love before another sun had set.'

'Winchester! So far?'

'I went to visit the bank where your papa deposited the money for you,' he told her. 'It was quite true that all of it was gone but when I spoke to the owner, showed him your letter and explained that we are to be married he disclosed the fact that your legal guardian, Thomas Hargreaves, had withdrawn the money in your name.' He sighed. 'It is as I thought, dearest. He has used your legacy to further his own business interests.'

She grasped his arm. 'And not only my money, Philip—he is using some of the children you yourself brought over from France as cheap labour in his mill!'

His eyes widened as he stared at her. 'But how can this be? And how do you know of it?'

As briefly as she could without leaving out any important details, she recounted the conversation she had overheard four nights ago. 'Monsieur Dupont is the 'Eagle',' she concluded. 'Or at least, the man who took his place. Oh, Philip, what can we do?'

He held her hands tightly. 'Listen, my love. Paul had not been able to discover much when I met him. The only contact he had has disappeared. But he did find out on his recent trip across the channel that the original 'Eagle' was Pierre Labeque. Yes, dearest, your own father. The man who took his place was in fact working for the revolutionaries—picking the bones of the victims like a vulture.'

205

'Monsieur Dupont,' Abigail said quietly, her eyes full of tears. 'I have often wondered what my papa's crime against the revolution was and now that I know I am very proud. But now I am even more determined to save the children, Philip.'

He nodded. 'Of course and I know that your father would be very proud of his brave daughter. My plan is this: that we leave tomorrow as though for the proposed visit to London, but instead we proceed north—to Lancashire.'

Abigail's eyes sparkled. 'Oh, yes! And when we have rescued the children we can take them to St. Dominic's. The Sisters there will care for them.' She looked at him solemnly. 'Will you tell your stepfather what we intend to do?'

He shook his head slowly. 'No. I think it will benefit us more to let him continue to live in his fool's paradise. Philip Jefferson the fop shall not be killed off quite yet.'

Remembering something, Abigail slipped her hand into her skirt pocket and brought out the patch-box, showing it to Philip.

'The other night he gave me this. He said it was a betrothal gift, but at the time of giving it he asked me if I would try to persuade you to take over the Manor so that he could retire to Lancashire. What do you suppose it means, Philip?'

He took the patch-box from her and examined it closely, then he looked at her, his eyes alight with excitement.

'It means, my love, that we have Thomas Hargreaves where we want him at last! This is part of a collection of jewellery I brought over some months ago with one of my charges. He has been gathering his own little hoard—a piece here and a piece there—and of course, he would never dream that you or I would recognize this!' He slapped his knee triumphantly. 'This is conclusive proof. It is all we need, Abigail. When faced with this there will be no escape for him!'

Her hand crept into his. 'But first the children, Philip. They must be safe first. We must say nothing till then.'

He smiled and kissed her. 'Of course. They shall have priority. We shall leave for the north tomorrow.'

CHAPTER TWELVE

Abigail lay quite still in the narrow little bed, listening to the regular breathing that told her Bess was asleep. Indeed she had fallen asleep as soon as she had lain her head down on the truckle bed in the tiny cell at the convent of St. Dominic and it was not surprising. They had travelled many miles since leaving Broomcott, Abigail herself was tired too, but much too excited to sleep.

Lying in the narrow, bare room she watched the shadowy patterns on the ceiling, following in her mind every step of their journey together: first to Dorchester by horseback, where, much to Bess's surprise and delight, they were joined by Jack, whom Philip had thought might be useful to them. From Dorchester to London by coach and from there to Manchester where Abigail had gazed in wonder at the closely packed houses, scurrying grey-faced people and loaded wagons that thronged the streets. Wat it possible, she had wondered, that people could live and survive in a place so devoid of beauty? But that was before Philip had taken her to Thomas Hargreaves's mill. Never in her life had she seen so many people working together in one place—men, women, children and machines packed tightly together in the hot, dust-laden atmosphere. Her eyes and throat had stung and smarted with the mist of fluff that filled the air and her head had reeled from the deafening noise of the clacking looms.

It had not taken them long to find the refugee children.

Most of them were crouched under the machinery, cleaning it even while it was in operation. Stopping machinery meant stopping production, they were told. Unable to speak English, they were bewildered and half starved, some of them sick with fear of all that went on around them and Abigail was dismayed to notice that many of them had half-healed injuries, some infected, caused no doubt by the machinery. The whole scene was like a nightmare and she was greatly relieved when at last Philip was able to convince the overseer that the children must be freed to go with them.

Together they had taken them to the inn where they were staying and, much to the astonishment of the landlord, Abigail and Bess had tended, bathed and fed them, finally putting them to bed on makeshift pallets in the room usually reserved for meetings. The following day Philip had hired a wagon and driver to take them all to Salisbury and St. Dominic's. They had made good progress, the new turnpike roads were a great improvement and the summer weather and long hours of daylight meant that they were able to travel for a good part of each day.

At the convent the Sisters had welcomed the children with open arms, just as Abigail had known they would. She had spent a long time with Mother Angela, telling her the story of their escape, then she had visited Sister Ursula and Sister Joseph at the orphanage. They had been so pleased to see her and to hear of her betrothal. Tomorrow she would rise early and hear Mass with them and then she and Philip would see Father Jeremy about blessing their marriage.

So much had happened that she had almost forgotten the confrontation with Thomas Hargreaves which faced them on their return. She dreaded it, but as long as the children were safe it was enough—for the present at any rate. She closed her eyes and thought of Philip. He and Jack were sleeping at Father Jeremy's presbytery. She had not spent a moment alone with him since their journey began and she longed for a few quiet minutes in his arms and the feel of his cheek against hers. But these were no thoughts to be thinking in her present surroundings, she chided herself, and, turning once more she managed to sleep at last.

Returning from Mass in the chapel next morning she found Bess dressing hurriedly, a look of shame on her face.

'Why didn't 'ee wake me, Miss Abi? Fair lazy you must think me, a'layin' 'ere till this hour!'

Abigail laughed. 'It is only six o'clock, Bess. I have been to early Mass and now Mr. Philip and I are to see Father Jeremy in the garden. There is no need for you to stir yet, the coach does not leave till eight.'

Bess looked at her helplessly. 'Surely there be something I can do, Miss Abi. I baint used to settin' about. My fingers'll grow idle-worms!'

Abigail laughed. 'Well, if you go to the kitchen I'm sure Sister Frances will welcome you,' she said, 'but if I were you I would rest.

Sarah will have plenty for you to do when we get back to Broomcott and we have had a tiring journey.'

The garden at St. Dominic's was wholly for the growing of vegetables and herbs with which to feed the hungry community the Sisters cared for and Abigail found Father Jeremy doing a little weeding while he waited for her. When he saw her coming along the dew—spangled grass path he straightened his back, a smile lighting his lined, rosy old face. What a beautiful young woman she had grown into. The Sisters could indeed be proud of her. The young man she was to marry was not a Catholic, it was true, but he was of stout heart and good character. He would bless their marriage as they desired and pray that God would guide them through life and show them the way to true happiness. He spoke to them in his gentle way and gave them good advice and Abigail thought deeply about it as they journeyed from Salisbury to Dorchester later that morning.

She and Philip sat close together in the coach, each silent with their own thoughts and plans till Philip suddenly said:

'If I am to take over the Manor I must do things my own way. It seems inevitable that enclosure will come, but I talked with Father Jeremy about it last night and he suggested that I should make the common land the property of the villagers. It shall be divided up

211

and each man shall be allotted a portion on which to grow food for his family. And there shall be work for all. I shall not turn the land over entirely to sheep as my stepfather intended.' He took her hand, looking into her eyes. 'I fear that war with France is coming, my love. We must grow food for the people.'

She sighed. 'Uncle Thomas will not like your plans.'

He drew in his lips grimly. 'There are a lot of things that he will like even less. But there is no choice. If he were not my stepfather I would see him in gaol for what he has done. As it is, he shall now dance to my tune as I have had to dance to his all these years.'

Abigail looked up at him. 'Philip—I have a favour to ask you. Bess and Jack would so much like to be married, but Bess's father will not agree because of Jack's parentage and his work as a fisherman. Perhaps if he were to work for you—'

He laughed and pressed her hand. 'It is already arranged my love. Jack is a good fellow and I agree with you that the sooner he and Bess are married the better. I have offered him work as groom. He is good with horses and as soon as we are settled I shall speak to Bess's father on his behalf.'

Her eyes shone. 'Oh, Philip, thank you, they will be so happy!' She glanced across to where the two young people sat close together, their fingers entwined, Bess's sleeping head on

212

Jack's broad shoulder, and breathed a happy sigh. 'You will not be sorry, darling,' she whispered. 'That I can promise you.'

The sun was low in the sky when the coach arrived at the King's Head. There had been delays on the way and they were glad to climb stiffly down and take refreshment at the inn. When they had rested they collected mounts from the livery stable and set forth on the last lap of the journey. All four were quiet during the ride, but when they came in sight of the sea and the great red ball of the sun setting into it, Jack said:

'Well—we'm home, thank God, and say what you will, there be no place like it.'

'Ah, you'm right, Jack,' Bess said with conviction. 'There's folks talkin' about movin' to the city to work but I say they wants to think again—an' I shall tell 'un so!'

Abigail silently endorsed their thoughts. She knew they were remembering the evil-smelling streets of Manchester and the life led by their inhabitants, their lungs choked by the dust-laden air and with hardly a glimpse of the sun to lighten their day. Gratefully, she breathed in the fresh tangy breeze from the sea.

Thomas Hargreaves awaited them in the drawingroom, a look of unsuspecting benevolence on his face.

'Well?' he said jovially. 'Was your visit successful?'

Philip strode into the centre of the room

213

and faced him. 'Yes, it was successful, though not, perhaps, in the way you mean,' he said sternly.

Thomas's expression changed from joviality to one of bewilderment.

'What do you mean?' he asked warily. 'What has happened?'

Philip closed the door and turned to look at his stepfather. 'Abigail tells me that it is your wish that I take over the Manor so that you can 'retire' to Manchester,' he said, his voice cold and brittle as ice.

Thomas nodded. 'That is right. I thought it was what you would wish now that you are about to be married. Surely you must now give up your life of pleasure-seeking?'

'You are a hypocrite!' Philip said. 'You know full well that you have inflamed the people of the village to such a pitch that you are now afraid of the consequences. You are running away and leaving me to deal with the wasps' nest you have stirred up.' He took a step forward, looking down at the frowning Thomas. 'But it is as well that you leave,' he said. 'It is as well that you go and attend to your business in Manchester—for you will find your workforce depleted!'

Thomas shook his head, thoroughly foxed by this new and totally unfamiliar Philip who faced him. 'What do you mean?' he barked. 'I don't know what the devil you're talking about!'

214

'You soon will!' Philip looked contemptuously down at him. 'The workforce of your mill is the poorer by twelve children—the twelve French refugee children you were using as cheap labour.' He watched as his stepfather crumpled, his face turning grey before his eyes as he groped for the arms of his chair and lowered himself slowly into it.

'How—how did you know?' he muttered. 'I—I don't understand—what have you done?'

'*Done?*' Philip thundered. 'What I have done is to take these poor, ill-used children to the safety that was promised them. After the suffering they had already endured I was surprised to find them still living.' He reached out his arm to Abigail who had been standing near the door and she came to his side. 'Abigail has been a great help to me in all this,' he said. 'Abigail—your niece and ward whose money you *stole* to make this infamy possible!'

Thomas rose up from his chair, his face a mask of startled fear. 'It is a pack of lies! Whoever told you this shall be punished!' His eyes narrowed. 'Was it that cheating snake Dupont?'

'No, it was not.' Philip pressed him back into the chair. 'Listen to me—*I* was the one who brought these children to safety across the channel. I risked my life on many occasions to bring them and their valuables out of the terror—only to find that you—my own stepfather—were abusing them and using their

215

money to further your own business. Stamping out all the good I thought I was doing!'

'It was not so—', Thomas blustered. 'I too was cheated—'

'Do not deny it. I recognized this—', Philip held the silver patch-box under his nose. 'And now I think you had better give me the rest,' he said quietly. 'It is needed for the children. I think you have harmed them enough.'

Thomas slumped in his chair, compressing his lips and drawing in a long, hissing breath. Then he rose to his feet and walked to the door. 'You had better come to the study,' he said resignedly.

The hoard was hidden behind a loose panel over the study fireplace and Thomas put all the jewellery he had filched on the desk, his face sagging despondently. When it was done and the panel replaced he looked at Philip.

'What are you going to do?' he asked, an edge of fear to his voice.

Philip looked at his stepfather for a long moment, then he said:

'I will tell you what I am going to do—I am going to take over as squire here as my father intended whilst you go back to Manchester where you belong, and you are going to pay Abigail back what you have stolen from her. And make no mistake, I have the exact figure from the bank, so make sure you do not default.'

Thomas opened his mouth as though to

216

speak, then he thought better of it and nodded, gulping hard. 'I have no choice but to do as you say,' he said bitterly.

Philip began to gather up the jewellery on the desk with Abigail's help and Thomas made his way to the door, but he had hardly reached it when the sound of a single shot broke the silence. Philip looked up sharply at Abigail and, dropping the jewellery back on to the table he strode out into the hall where he almost collided with Bess as she came running from the kitchen.

'Oh, sir—Mr. Philip—Miss Abi!' she spluttered. 'There be trouble in the cove. Jed do say as the excise men've caught a boatful of men an' goods. It seems that someone give 'em the tip, like.'

'Smugglers?' Abigail asked.

Bess nodded, her eyes wide with fear. ' 'Tis likely there'll be more taken from Mortstone—you don't think my Jack—'

'No!' Philip took her by the shoulders. 'I know that Jack had nothing to do with anything of that sort. Besides, he was with us not an hour since. We must go and see if he needs us.' He hurried out of the house with Abigail following. It was very dark now but as they neared the cliffs the sound of more shots and the babble of confusion came to them from the direction of the cove. Abigail grasped Philip's arm.

'It sounds as though they are taken. I hope
217

there are no men from the village. They have been sorely pressed for money of late, it would not surprise me if—' She broke off as two shadowy figures appeared ahead of them. Philip hailed them:

'Hello, there! Do you know what is happening?'

Both figures spun round just as Bess came running with a lantern. As she held it aloft they saw to their surprise that they were looking into the faces of Miles and Rebecca Wilford. Two pairs of eyes stared bemusedly at them for a moment before Rebecca spoke:

'It is smugglers—at least, so we believe. It seems they are putting up a fight. But where have *you* come from?'

'We have only just returned from our travels,' Abigail explained. 'We heard the shots and came to see.'

Brother and sister stared at each other speechlessly but at that moment running footsteps heralded the arrival of someone else. Bess held the lantern high and gave a cry of relief as she recognized Jack.

'Oh, thank the dear Lord you'm safe,' she cried. 'What be goin' on, fer pity's sake?'

He stood for a moment, struggling for breath, then he said, addressing himself to Philip: 'Sir—it were you I were a'comin' for. They been to the Dolphin—the excise men— an' they'm taken some men from the back room. I 'eard 'em say as 'ow they'd got the ringleader, sir. But I saw the man as they took 'im away and t'was—t'was—' He glanced apprehensively at Miles and Rebecca and Miles dug him sharply in the ribs.

'Go on, Fellow—we're all law-abiding people—who was it?'

Jack gulped. ' 'Twere your father, sir— 'twere Parson Wilford: Him the fishermen called 'Holy Willie'.'

For a moment there was a stunned silence as they all stared at each other. Then Rebecca let out a shrill scream, turning wildly on her brother, beating into him with both fists.

'*Aaah!* This is all your fault! You *idiot*! Oh, how shall we ever live down the disgrace? Oh, no—*no*—*no*!' And sobbing hysterically she ran off into the darkness with her brother in hot pursuit.

It was then that Abigail heard the sound. It was something she had never heard before, nor ever thought she would hear. Standing just behind them where he had arrived in time to hear Jack's revelation and the Wilfords' reaction to it, Thomas Hargreaves was *laughing*—his hands to his sides and the tears rolling down his cheeks.

'Parson Wilford—oh, that's rich,' he wheezed. 'It almost makes everything worth while. Parson Wilford—*Holy Willie!* Oh, dear me!'

*   *   *

Abigail and Philip stood hand in hand on the clifftop watching the sunset. A week had passed since their return from Manchester. Thomas Hargreaves had departed the following morning declaring that he intended never to set foot in Broomcott again. Immediately Philip had arranged a meeting for the men of the village to make clear to them his plans for the future. Now all that remained was their wedding, which was to take place tomorrow.

Philip swung Abigail round to face him. 'Well, my love. This time tomorrow you will be Mrs. Philip Jefferson.' His eyes twinkled mischievously. 'Yet once you told me you did not and *never could* love the man to whom you were betrothed. Do you remember?'

She laughed up at him. 'There are other things I remember saying too—before I knew that you were that man.'

He drew her close. 'I like to remember you saying that you wanted to bear my children. It is a moment I cherish.' He raised her face to his with one finger, looking into her eyes tenderly. 'I shall be so proud to make you my wife, darling. How many children will you bear me?' He kissed her softly.

'As many as you like,' she laughed, her cheeks pink. 'Who can tell? I only know one thing for sure.'

He smiled down at her. 'And what is that?'

'Why, that the first boy will be called Roget and the first girl, Jenny,' she said.

They looked down into the cove where the incoming tide gently lapped the beach with white-edged wavelets.

'Who could have thought such violence occurred down there only a few nights ago,' Philip said thoughtfully. 'I only thank God that no one was killed.'

But Abigail's eyes were on the horizon. 'And on the other side of the water it still goes on,' she sighed. 'With war to come, so everyone says.' She looked up at him. 'Oh Philip, will peace ever come to France again?' She shuddered and he put an arm round her waist, drawing her close to his side.

'One day, dearest. In the meantime we will do all that we can to help the unfortunate innocents.' He lifted her face between his hands and kissed her deeply. 'Always remember that our love came out of that chaos and while that can happen there must always be hope.'

Arms linked, they walked slowly back towards the Manor, each looking forward to tomorrow—and to the rest of their life together.

We hope you have enjoyed this Large Print book. Other Chivers Press or Thorndike Press Large Print books are available at your library or directly from the publishers.

For more information about current and forthcoming titles, please call or write, without obligation, to:

Chivers Press Limited
Windsor Bridge Road
Bath BA2 3AX
England
Tel. (01225) 335336

OR

Thorndike Press
P.O. Box 159
Thorndike, Maine 04986
USA
Tel. (800) 223-2336

All our Large Print titles are designed for easy reading, and all our books are made to last.